Diamondz Are Forever

By
Monique Marshall

PublishAmerica
Baltimore

ISBN: 1-60703-541-3
PUBLISHED BY PUBLISHAMERICA, LLLP
www.publishamerica.com
Baltimore

Printed in the United States of America

Dedication

This book is dedicated to the most important people in my life: God, for giving me the gift of written word and expression; to my mother for giving all of herself so that I may live; to the loving memory of my sister, Charnika Joynes, may God bless her soul; to my husband and daughters for making me whole; and to my big brother for making the sacrifices that allowed me to be educated and free.

Diamondz
Are Forever

Chapter 1

It's 1996, and sixteen-year-old Diamond is sitting on her front porch watching the cars drive by. Her older brother, Junior, is outside with his friends, Jake and P, and her mother, Lynne, is at work. Her father is not at home; he remarried years ago and stopped coming around. Junior, eight years her senior, is the family protector and provider. With ten toes down and running, he makes more money in one day than Lynne makes in a week.

"Hey, ya'll ready to roll out? I got some people waiting down the street," Jake asked.

"Naw, ya'll go ahead. I gotta wait for my mom to get home before I go out," Junior replied.

"Okay, that's cool, see you later tonight," Jake said as he walked off.

"Yeah, see ya," Junior said. Diamond watched as Jake and P walked down the block towards Steel City, a housing project where drugs were openly sold. Junior walked up the front porch steps and into the house. Diamond followed.

"I'm hungry," she said.

"So go cook," Junior replied.

"Mommy gotta get groceries. Can I drive to McDonald's?" she asked.

"Go straight there and back—no side stops or that's your ass!" Junior replied as he tossed the keys to his 1995 gold Lexus.

"Thanks. I'm going to eat there and then come home so my food won't get cold," she said as she grabbed her purse from the couch and walked out the front door.

Diamond hopped into the car and adjusted the seat and mirrors. She thought to herself, "I think I'll take the long way so that I can see who is outside."

She drove straight two blocks to Steel City to see what dope boys were working the day shift. She drove past dilapidated houses that were burned by fire and never completely knocked down, brick project buildings with busted windows, and an open field where kids were playing football. She watched the little kids playing in front of the buildings, and the dope fiends walking swiftly by to put money in the hands of the boys serving out front. She made a right turn and drove down a steep hill towards the old steel mills.

The steel mills were the lifeblood and pride of the city ten years ago, but stand as relics of a city now claimed by crack cocaine, guns, and violence. She made a right turn up Washington Street, the main strip, to see if any of her friends were out. The corner store was buzzing with young people in and out; the bar was open with old heads out front watching as the young girls walk by.

Young men with pit bull dogs stood on the corner dancing to the music of cars riding by. Diamond made a right onto Central Avenue and drove past the park where her friends might be.

"Hey, girl," Marie yelled as she saw Diamond approaching. Diamond parked in front of the park to talk to Marie.

"Hey, girl, what's up?" Diamond asked with a smile.

"Not much, watching the fellas play ball—chillin' actually. Where you going?" Marie asked.

"To Mickie D's to eat, you wanna come?" Diamond asked.

"Naw, I'm waiting for Eric to get done playing so I can go to his house before his mom gets off work," Marie said with a devious look on her face.

"Girl, you better be careful sneaking around; your mom and his mom are going to get you," Diamond warned.

"You sound like my mom. Hey, I'll see you later, okay," Marie said as she ran back to the park to join the girls on the bench watching the basketball game.

Diamond knows the streets; she listens when Junior tells her about how to read people and how to deal with people fairly, but always with caution. Diamond watches how Junior treats his women and takes notes. She absorbs the good and the bad that come with the street life: the police, the fights, the guns, and the smell of crack cooking in the kitchen when she gets home unexpectedly. She tries to separate herself from the fast-tail girls who sneak with the older boys to have sex; and she definitely avoids the grown men who prey on the young girls. She is sad for the women crack addicts who beg and plead for crumbs from the dope boys, and exchange their bodies for a hit. But she is happy for her brother, who has been lucky to go outside, get money, and come home in one piece.

Chapter 2

It's mid-August 1997. Diamond is a senior at Valley High School. She pulls up to the student parking lot behind the school and parks her new navy blue Chevy Tahoe. The music blasts as she turns off her truck and smiles at herself in the rearview mirror. She is physically FINE, five feet and six inches tall, with a slim waist and thick legs. She's light skinned, the product of a black father and an Italian mother, with long, black, curly hair. She is at the top of her class in academics, and is very athletic. To put icing on the cake, Diamond is "dope girl fresh."

She enters Valley High School for the first day of school. She walks down the hall and enters room 214, her homeroom, and takes a seat in the front row, as she always does. Diamond is the only student in the room when a group of three Italian boys walk in. Benny, Scott, and Chris have been in class with Diamond since third grade. She is intelligent, and her classmates are the top students in the graduating class of 1998. Benny takes the seat next to her and smiles. "What's up, sweets?" he asked.

"Not much," Diamond replied.

Benny and Diamond have dated on and off since middle school, but because Diamond is half-black, the relationship is forbidden and private. His father is a teacher and football coach at the high school, and his mother works in the front office. The irony of the situation is that as much as his parents are against it, he loves her. He visits her at her house, takes her places outside the city, buys her bracelets, writes her love letters, and studies with her in class. They challenge each other and are good friends.

"Not much. How are you?" she asked.

Suddenly, Ron, a tall, thin, dark-skinned teenage boy enters the room and says, "Good morning, sunshine."

Ron is one of Diamond's best male friends. Ron and Diamond share the same godfather, Uncle Pete, and were raised as cousins. They were taught to watch out for each other and to be the best of friends. Ron's mother, Lynette, and Diamond's mother, Lynne, were close friends, so Diamond often called Ron's mother "mommy" because they were considered to be family.

"I want to know if you would like to go out to eat with me and the fellas later tonight," Ron asked.

"Sure, love. What time?" Diamond replied.

"About 6:30 p.m., right after football practice," Ron said.

Just then the school bell rang and Ron darts out of the classroom. The faces that enter the room are all familiar, since most of the students have been together since elementary school. Kalin takes the seat next to Diamond, smiles, and asks, "What's up, lady?"

"Not much. Ready for our last year of school?" Diamond responded.

"You know I'm ready, girlfriend; we are almost grown, thank God!" Kalin replied.

Kalin is Diamond's best female friend. She is cocoa brown, with thick black eyebrows. She looks a lot like a young Lauryn Hill. Slim and shapely, Kalin too is very intelligent and often partners with Diamond on school assignments and projects. Kalin's parents are churchgoers and as a result, Kalin has strong moral values.

Diamond admires Kalin's ability to blend with a crowd and have fun, and always manage to separate herself from the crowd when she has to. Kalin always encourages Diamond to be her best self and never acts high and mighty towards others. On the other hand, Kalin admires Diamond's intelligence and personality. Diamond knows how to make other people feel good about themselves, by actively listening and engaging in good conversation. Diamond is skilled at seeing the positive characteristics in people, and often pays compliments to others. Diamond can also be manipulative and seductive when she needs to be.

Chapter 3

Diamond pulls up to the restaurant at 6:45 p.m., fashionably late. She enters the spot with a knee-length denim skirt, light pink sandals, and a pink and white shirt. Her pink Coach purse and belt make the outfit complete. Ron waves to her from across the room and jumps up to greet her. "Hey, sunshine, glad you made it." Ron said.

"Hey, Ron, looks like ya'll having fun," Diamond replied.

"Come on, I want you to meet someone," Ron said as he grabs her hand and leads her to the table. "Sunshine, you already know my crew, Aaron and Tre, and of course you know Moe; but I want you to meet Champ, Moe's cousin from down south," Ron said as he points to everyone around the table, and stops at a caramel-skinned, handsome man. Diamond's eyes halt as she quickly scans Champ's face. He has a full beard and mustache; a scar that looks like a razor blade cut ran across his right cheek; and a beauty mark on his nose. He has a fitted baseball hat on, but Diamond can tell he has a low fade haircut. Champ is a show stopper, and Diamond likes him immediately.

"Hello, Diamond," Moe said. Diamond snaps out of her stare, and turns her attention to Moe.

"What up?" Diamond replies in a dry tone of voice. Diamond cannot stand the sight of Moe. She dated him for her entire sophomore year, and her skin crawls every time she sees him. The truth is that Diamond was deeply in love with Moe and got pregnant about six months into the relationship. Teenage pregnancy was not in the plan for Diamond, so at the age of fifteen, she had an abortion. Diamond quickly turned the love that she had for Moe into anger. After Diamond broke up with Moe, she despised him in order to deal with her pain.

"Champ, huh?" Diamond asks as she extends her hand to shake his.

"Yes, my name is Champion and I'm happy to meet you, Diamond," he said as he reaches to shake her hand firmly. Diamond's heart flutters, she was no fool, she knows she likes Champ, and he knows it too.

Diamond flirts, "Well, Champ, I hope to see you around." She smiles and winks her eye at him as she walks away to sit next to Ron.

The fellas talked about their usual topics: whose girlfriend is the hottest, football practice, new brand-name clothes, shoes, etc. Diamond is bored listening to their conversation so she excuses herself from the table and walks to the restroom. Inside the bathroom, she inspects herself in the mirror, fixes her clothes, and applies cherry-flavored lip gloss. She pops a fresh piece of gum into her mouth and walks out of the restroom. She returns to the table to find the waiter bringing out the food. She sits down and enjoys a chicken salad, with ranch dressing and ice water. The fellas talk and laugh, while she sits and listens. She prefers the company of males over females and is often asked her opinion by the fellas who have girlfriend problems or need help with their school work. She watches Champ as he talks to Moe and laughs with the fellas. He catches her staring and she smiles.

"Hey, guys, it's been real, but I have to get my beauty sleep, so I'll see you all tomorrow at school," Diamond says aloud as she stands up to leave.

"Oh, let me walk you outside then," Ron said as he stood up.

"Okay. Be safe, fellas," Diamond said as she walks toward the exit.

Ron walks her to her truck, says good-bye, and runs back inside the restaurant to finish hanging out with the fellas. Diamond sits in her truck thinking, "Make a move or not? I want Champ bad! He is sexy and caramel. He has a beauty mark on his face, and a scar. He seems like a double-edged sword, attractive and healthy, but maybe a darker side, scarred and dangerous."

Diamond has it bad; she loves men. She is spoiled by her brother; seventeen years old with a brand-new truck, new clothes, and new shoes. She takes a deep breath and knows Champ will be her poison, her fix; she is addicted, and she doesn't even know him yet. As Moe and Champ exit the restaurant door to leave, Diamond pulls off, with the music blasting.

Chapter 4

Champ is a double-edged sword. He is good-hearted, determined, and intelligent. He is a country boy at heart and grew up in the mountains of West Virginia. He loves dogs, especially pit bulls, and likes to ride four-wheelers and dirt bikes through the mountain trails. He swims and is an athlete. Calvin, five years younger than Champ, follows his brother closely. As children, whenever Champ went out to swim or play basketball, he took Calvin along. Champ loved his little brother and took good care of him. Both Champ and Calvin were happy children, but all good things came to an end when their mother left.

Champ's mother, Irene, abandoned her sons when Champ was twelve years old. Irene is a sexy, high yellow woman. She is the product of a black mother and a full-blooded Native American father. Her eyes are green and her hair is long and silky. Irene is good with numbers, and in order to become an accountant, she decided to leave her two sons behind. Irene left

Champ and his little brother, Calvin, with her sister Angela and moved to South Carolina.

Auntie Angela is a God-fearing woman who loves to cook. She too is beautiful, but she is married to a fake preacher, Uncle Von. Uncle Von has his own church and is the town mayor. He is a jealous man and often argues with his wife for spoiling Champ and Calvin. Angela loves her nephews and does all that she can to shower them with affection, but as much as she tries, her husband makes life hell for the boys.

Auntie Layla, Moe's mother, is Champ's favorite aunt. She too fears God, but as a young woman she ran the streets. She works hard as a nurse during the day, and enjoys the night life after work. She too is high yellow with hazel eyes and long brown hair. She is a confident woman and has no problem getting the attention of any man that she wants. Her honesty won Champ's heart. She talks to him about life and his feelings, she listens to him when he is happy and sad, and she takes up for him when anyone wrongs him. She became his mother and he honors her as such.

Throughout high school, Champ played basketball and was an all-American star. He scored an average of twenty points per game his freshman and sophomore years. His junior year, Champ was observed by college coaches and scouts. He received many basketball scholarship offer letters in the mail and attended several college tours with the hope of being recruited to play at a Division I school.

Uncle Von was extremely jealous of Champ's athletic abilities and popularity, and the summer before his senior year, he forbid

Champ from playing basketball. Champ's coaches tried to convince Uncle Von that Champ was college bound and that he could get a full scholarship as long as he played well his senior year, but Uncle Von refused. Champ was furious because his mother left Uncle Von and Aunt Angela to be his legal guardians and Aunt Angela would not go against her husband to help Champ stay on the team. For the sake of his younger brother Calvin, Champ pushed forward and graduated from high school with advanced math honors.

After graduation, Champ evaluated his situation and knew that he should be in college on a full basketball scholarship. But his reality was harsh, his estranged mother could not provide a place for both him and his brother Calvin, and the need for money and a place of his own were obligations that he had to meet. Champ decided to move out of his uncle's house and was on his own. Irene came to get Calvin, and without basketball or the option for a free ride to college, Champ took to the streets and drug dealing became his occupation.

When Champ started his adult life he had a cold heart towards women and fools. He used his personality and intelligence to maneuver the streets and find out who the money man was. Once he determined that the money man was local, Champ established a connection with him and started his career by traveling from state to state delivering any amount of dope, guns, and money. At any given time he could pull out thousands of dollars and he was nice with conversation, a salesman. He could sell milk to a cow, he was so slick with is tongue. Champ was a pimp, and drugs were his hoes. He had cocaine, ecstasy, and hydro for sale.

Champ is a weed connoisseur and takes pride in only selling the finest buds. He traveled first class, a black Chevy Tahoe for work, and a navy Benz for pleasure. The whole time he was living large, he was empty inside. He wanted someone to share his life with and to be intimate with, but he trusted no woman and he played many. He had game and he wasn't afraid to show it, all the while he had a protective wall up with a deep desire to love and be loved.

Chapter 5

On June 6, 1998, Diamond graduates from Valley High School third in her class. The graduation party is a huge block party at the park in Steel City. The scene is live when Diamond and Kalin pull up. Diamond parks the truck and hops out looking like a model. She has on a short khaki skirt with a yellow strapless shirt, and yellow high-heel shoes. Diamond's long, black hair flows straight down her back. Kalin wears a fitted, khaki one-piece dress with brown-and-khaki-colored sandals. Diamond and Kalin are immediately greeted by classmates and friends as they join the party. Diamond and Kalin hit the dance floor and jam to the music. As Diamond and Kalin laugh and dance, Champ walks up behind Diamond and asks, "Can I speak to you in private?"

"Sure," Diamond said and gives Kalin a hand signal. She follows him off the dance floor.

He slows down to extend his hand to Diamond. She grabs hold of his hand and allows him to lead her to his car. Diamond's heart pounds in her chest, but she appears calm and continues to follow his lead. Champ opens the car door for her, and she sits down in the front seat of his car. It is the navy Benz tonight, and Diamond is glad to be in it.

Champ looks directly in Diamond's eyes and asks her, "Can I do something special for you tonight? I've been watching you since we met at the restaurant and I want to show my appreciation to you for being a beautiful, intelligent woman."

Diamond blushes and responds, "Yes, you can."

Champ starts the car and Biggie Smalls came blasting through the speakers. He turns a few corners to a quiet spot and pulls over. He turns the music off and looks at Diamond. For the first time, Diamond is speechless. She doesn't know what to do or say; at that moment she is open and vulnerable to his magic. He pulls out a box from the back seat and hands it to Diamond. She takes it and said, "Thank you, but you hardly know me to give me a gift."

He looks serious and straight into her eyes, and said, "I want to get to know you; I've heard great things about you. You deserve the gift for being beautiful inside and out."

Diamond takes a deep breath and opens the box. Her jaw drops in surprise as she finds a shiny diamond bracelet. The blue and yellow diamonds are the same color as her high school team colors. She leans forward and places her hand on his chin. She moves her fingers over his face. Diamond loves him and she doesn't even know him. He grabs her hands and guides them to his heart. He moves her hands to his mouth and kisses each one of her fingertips.

Diamond is gone, she is in heaven. She is helpless, and she

loves the feeling. He asked her, "Diamond, will you stay with me tonight? You know I hustle for a living, but let me show you who I am. For some reason I trust you, and I trust no one. You remind me of my auntie, and she is a special lady."

Diamond takes a deep breath and said, "I've wanted you since the first time I saw you. I got a funny feeling, and I like it. You're right, I do know what you do. I live in that world too, selling dope, making money, and moving all the time. I have goals and dreams and I can't promise anything. But yes, I'll stay with you tonight."

Champ moves into Diamond's space, pulls her close, and gives her a long, slow, passionate kiss from a man to a woman. That kiss seals her fate; she has to have that good feeling always. Diamond's body caught fire; she is thinking so many different things: "What will I do if I fall in love?" "What will my brother say?" "Are we going to make love tonight?"

Champ leans back in the driver's seat and said, "Diamond, I know you are the sister of a hustler and that he will kill for you. I also know that you are only seventeen years old and that your birthday is in September."

Diamond was happy to know that he had taken the time to do a little research on her, and said, "You've done your homework on me, that's good! What else do you know about me?"

Champ smiled. "I know that you used to love my cousin Moe and that you two have been broke up for about two years now. Moe still talks about you and I think he's going to be mad when he finds out that you are my woman now."

"Your woman? Sweetheart, I am my own woman," Diamond asked with a little attitude.

"Yes, in due time you will be mine," he said with confidence.

Diamond couldn't believe what was happening to her. Champ read her mind; just as she asked herself questions, he gave her answers. Diamond felt like she was under his spell, like he knew just what to say to let her know that he was serious. Diamond turned to him and said, "Thank you for the gift and the kiss. I'm feeling you too, but I need a few minutes to think. I want to go with you, but I'm not sure what it would mean."

Champ could sense that she was nervous. He knew Diamond wasn't a virgin, and that the two boys that she slept with in high school were long-term relationships, not one-night stands. Champ had taken the time to ask about Diamond, so he said to her, "I'll give you the key; it's room 330 at the Radisson. Go back to the party and celebrate with your friends. I will be at the room when you get there."

Diamond nodded her head and whispered, "Thanks."

Champ drove Diamond back to the party, and as she opened the door to get out of the car, he said, "I know I'm asking a lot of you, Diamond, and that you have big plans for your future. I don't want to change any of that; in fact, I want to be a part of all of it."

Diamond leaned over, kissed him, and said, "I'll see you in a little while, Champion. Thanks."

Chapter 6

Diamond pulls into the Radisson Hotel parking lot at 2:00 a.m., and the block party is just ending. She danced and shared the excitement of graduation with her classmates. Benny asked her to call him when she got home, but Diamond refused. She knew she wasn't going home tonight.

Diamond parks her truck, turns off the motor, and sits quietly. She closes her eyes and prays, "God, thank you for today, thank you for my life and for my safety. Please protect me and lead me. Tell me if Champ is the one man for me. Amen."

With that prayer, Diamond let go, took a deep breath and got out of her truck. She felt more alive than she has ever felt. She is excited and looks forward to whatever Champ has in store for her. She enters the main lobby of the Radisson and walks towards the elevators. She has been to the hotel many times before for sports banquets and academic conferences for school. But she has never been an overnight guest with a man before, and just the thought of it makes her feel grown up.

Diamond enters the elevator and rides quietly to the third floor. She has butterflies in her stomach, and she laughs at herself for being so nervous. It's not like she's never been with a man before. She loved Moe and explored his body from head to toe several times during their relationship. After she left Moe, she hurt and looked for love elsewhere. Elsewhere turned out to be a classmate and one of the fellas: Rob.

The elevator door opens and Diamond exits and walks towards the room. She stops in front of the door marked 330 and knocks. No answer, so Diamond uses her key and opens the door. She is greeted by the smell of fresh roses. There are petals all over the floor and a trail leading to the couch. The room is a hotel suite so there are two levels. The downstairs has a couch, a big-screen TV, a desk area, and a patio door that leads to a pool-side view. Diamond follows the trail of petals to the couch to find a note that read:

"I'M HAPPY YOU'RE HERE. COME UPSTAIRS."

Diamond obeys and walks up the steps. Upstairs is a king-size bed, a huge Jacuzzi surrounded by mirrors, a fireplace, a walk-in closet, and a bathroom. Diamond notices another note on the Jacuzzi. The note read:

"LOOK IN THE CLOSET."

She walks to the closet and opens the door. Inside, she finds two beautiful Victoria's Secret pajama sets, not seductive lingerie, but two pink tank tops and two pair of white boy shorts. Attached to one of the hangers is another note.

"TAKE A SHOWER, TRY THESE ON, I'LL BE THERE SOON."

Diamond follows the directions, and takes a warm shower. The water is lovely and relaxing. She prays again, "Dear God, I know I am not married and here with this man. But, God, he is so beautiful and he is yours. Please let your will be done. Keep me safe and get me home. Amen."

She gets out of the shower, lotions her body, and slips into the size-small outfit. As she exits the steamy bathroom, she can smell blueberries in the air. She walks downstairs to greet Champ. He is sitting on the couch, smoking a blunt, when she enters the room. He sits up and fixes his eyes on her.

"Wow, lil' momma, you look beautiful!" Champ said with a smile.

Diamond knows how to be seductive and wants to please him for treating her so special. Diamond sits on his lap and puts both of her hands on his face. She kisses him and he kisses her back. Diamond straddles him and Champ rubs her back and ass. He whispers in her ear,

"I want to taste you."

Diamond gets up and leads Champ up the steps to the bed. She takes off her pajamas and lies on the bed. Champ takes off his shirt and begins kissing Diamond's stomach. He moves down slow and kisses her thighs and waist. Diamond is in ecstasy; Champ is in control, and she submits to him. He kisses, sucks, licks, and tastes Diamond. He uses his hands and mouth to touch and taste every inch of her body. He works hard to please her. Diamond is grateful and reaches her climax. She lets out a deep moan as Champ flicks his tongue gently over her clit. Diamond's body shakes; she is wide open and wants him bad. Diamond sits up and says, "Thank you, love, but now I want to please you."

It is her turn, and she is going to be free. Champ takes off his shoes and jeans. He slides two condoms under the pillow and lies down on the bed. Diamond climbs on top of him and kisses his lips. She moves down and kisses his neck and chest. Diamond touches Champ all over and said, "I want you."

Champ reaches for a condom and put it on. Diamond can feel every inch of him as she mounts him. She lets out deep moans as she moves up and down and feels him inside of her. He holds both of her hands as she rides him. They are connected emotionally and physically, and they enjoy each other. Together they make passionate love and fall asleep satisfied, wrapped up in each other.

Diamond wakes up at 10:30 a.m. and rolled over. Champ is still asleep, so Diamond slipped out of bed and went to the bathroom. In the bathroom, she looked at herself in the mirror. She is complete. She graduated at the top of her class; she is going to college in the fall. She is attractive and now she has a man to complement her. She feels confident, and thanks God for sending Champion to her.

Chapter 7

Diamond and Champ see each other as much as they can. He is working, making at least $20,000 a month. He has a house outside of the city where he lives alone and a dope house in the city on the south side of town. Valley is jumping for drugs and the party scene.

Diamond's house is exactly one block from Champ's trap house. She walks the same ground that pipe heads occupy on a daily basis. The trap house functioned like a McDonald's drive-thru. A fiend will pull up, place an order, and drive off a satisfied customer. The menu includes cocaine, pills, and the highest quality weed.

Champ runs a tight operation and never keeps drugs in the house. He keeps a yard full of pit bulls and a six-foot-tall wooden fence that encloses the entire house. The work is in one dog house and the money in another. The house itself is situated at the corner of a main road and a side street, but it sits back far enough to see what cars are coming and going.

There is no vehicle traffic directly to the house; corner boys and workers are posted on all corners within a one-block radius. Customers are served in their cars by young boys in white t-shirts and jeans. Champ's young boys have the block on lock and the police know it. Champ lays low and he never goes to the house during work hours. Money and product are moved in the middle of the night and never in large amounts in case of a robbery or bust.

Diamond and Champ keep their relationship a secret for many reasons. Primarily because Junior, Diamond's brother, will not approve and will react violently to the news. Junior and Diamond made an agreement when Diamond entered her freshman year of high school: Junior will deposit $1,000 per month into a college fund for her as long as she agrees to get straight A's on her report card, stay out of the streets, go to college to study pre-law, and NEVER DATE A HUSTLER!

Diamond is in direct violation of the agreement when she is with Champ, and she doesn't want to make Junior mad. More importantly, Champ is under federal investigation for drug trafficking and money laundering, and Diamond does not want to be involved.

Diamond and Champ spend their summer celebrating Diamond's graduation and their new relationship together by taking trips and traveling. The couple visit California, New York, and the Bahamas in June and July 1998. In August, they spend time in Miami and Atlanta. They talk about future goals and plans, having children, and getting out of the drug game. It is a picture-perfect relationship, but time is winding down to when Diamond will have to leave for college.

She doesn't want to let Champ go, but she knows that in order to go to school and do well, she has to leave him alone. Diamond cannot be distracted or worried about him, so she makes the hardest decision of her life, and separates herself from him. It is a temporary split, she tells herself, in order to avoid the pain and anxiety of losing her love. Nonetheless, Champ understands it for exactly what it is: a breakup. Diamond has to move on, and he knows it. Diamond feels like she is stuck between two worlds: her relationship with Champ and the fun and excitement of love versus her future as a lawyer and all of the opportunities that being a lawyer will bring. Diamond has to shake Champ, but it will not be easy.

Chapter 8

Diamond, Lynne, and Junior pull up to Indiana University with a U-haul full of brand-new furniture and clothing. Diamond and Junior have visited the campus twice before to tour and rent the two-bedroom townhouse that Diamond will occupy for her first year of college. Junior has paid Diamond's rent six months in advance so that she will have no worries while at school.

When Lynne and Junior open the front door, reality set in, and Diamond starts to cry.

"What the hell you crying for?" shouted Junior.

"I'm just glad we made it! You and Ma have sacrificed so much for me to be here and I am thankful." Diamond sobs.

Lynne comforts her daughter and said, "You will be able to help so many people when you become a lawyer. We have invested in you because we believe that you will do great things."

Diamond walks into her new home. Lynne and Junior follow. Diamond takes both of their hands and asks, "Can we pray?" Junior and Lynne bow their heads as Diamond takes a deep breath and prays, "God, thank you for today. Thank you for continuing to keep my family safe. Thank you for the sacrifice that was made to get me here today. Please, God, guide and protect me as I begin the journey into adult life. Help me to help others. Amen." With that prayer, Diamond let go of the fear and anxiety.

Junior makes a phone call to someone he knows in the area to come and help unload the U-haul. About fifteen minutes later two young, attractive white men pull up in an old white Ford Bronco. Junior introduces the driver, a tall, thick Italian man with dark brown hair and dark brown eyes. His name is Jack. The passenger looks like the driver, only younger. His name is Brice.

Junior pulls Diamond next to him and walks to the window of the passenger side of the truck and said, "Diamond, meet your cousins, Jack and Brice. Guys, this is my baby sister Diamond." Both men get out of the truck and extend their hands to greet Diamond. Lynne walks over and hugs the two men.

Lynne explains, "These two fine young men are the children of my favorite cousin, Kim. Kim moved from Valley right after she graduated from high school twenty years ago. Cousin Kim and her family live close by and will be available to help you get settled, Diamond."

"Pleased to meet you guys," Diamond responds. She had no idea that she had family so close to her new college, but she is happy that between school, work, and learning her way around the new city, that she will be able to take her mind off Champ.

Junior, Jack, and Brice unload the U-haul, while Diamond and

Lynne go inside to clean and inspect the townhouse. Lynne looks at Diamond and said, "I'm really proud of you, baby. Your brother is very intelligent too, but he chose to make money to support us, rather than go to college. You are not like him, you have a chance to be free and learn so much. Separate yourself from the streets, and you will succeed."

Diamond nodded her head in agreement. Lynne has spoken to Diamond all of her life about rising above the madness of the streets, and constantly encourages Diamond to separate herself. The irony of her life is that the one person that she wants to make her life complete is heavy in the streets, and she knows he is off-limits: Champ.

After the men unload the truck, Jack and Brice give Diamond their address and phone numbers. Lynne and Junior have a long drive ahead, and are ready to leave Diamond at college. Just before they get into the U-haul truck, Junior gives Diamond a large, white envelope and she looks inside. There is $500 cash and a bank book.

"What's this?" Diamond asked.

"It's your college fund. You did what I asked you to do. You have $36,000 to spend over the next four years. I'm not cutting you off, I'll always help you out, but you are an adult now. You are off to a wonderful start, now finish what we started," Junior said. Diamond runs to her brother and jumps into his arms.

She kisses him and said, "Thank you. I won't let you down."

The family said their final good-byes, and Diamond walks inside of her new home. She sits on the couch and looks around:

new college, new home, new furniture, new clothes, and a brand-new life. Diamond is grateful, yet sad. She is happy to be away from the poverty and drugs, but she misses Champ terribly. It has been two weeks since she has seen him, and she wonders how he is doing.

Chapter 9

Back in Valley, Champ is full speed ahead. He thinks about Diamond every day, but he has bigger problems to worry about. Champ's closest men were arrested by the feds in a drug raid at a trap house out of town. Since no drugs or money were in the house, the men were charged with concealing a weapon, and illegal possession of firearms equipment for having bulletproof vests on. The raid forced Champ to shut down his operation, which had a ripple effect on the drug trade in the city. In order to keep himself safe, Champ decided to get rid of the rest of the drugs that he has without contacting anyone that he has done business with previously. The FBI is closing in on Champ, and he knows it.

Champ decides to take a vacation and travels to Atlantic City to gamble. He travels alone since Diamond is gone. He misses having her around. They are friends and lovers. He enjoys lying on the pillow next to her at night and sharing his deepest thoughts and desires. He trusts her and he knows that one day she will be his wife. He thought about giving the street life up and going to live with her, but he doesn't want to bring the problems that he has created to her world.

Champ is at the bar of his hotel when he notices a pretty, light-skinned woman at the table across the room. He can't help staring because he feels like he has seen her face before. He watches her, as she picks up her drink and walks to the dance floor. Although he loves Diamond and would never intentionally hurt her, he is no fool and he puts his life on hold for no one.

The woman looks Hispanic, her hair is long and dark brown, and her facial features are beautiful. She is petite and wears a short yellow dress with yellow heels. She has diamonds in her ears, on her neck, and on her wrist. She obviously is well taken care of. Just then, it clicks. He has done business with this woman before. Six months ago on an out-of-town trip to Texas, that same face picked up the money and delivered the cocaine to him. But that woman had a tattoo on her right wrist that read "BEAUTIFUL," and he had to know if it was her. Champ walked over to the dance floor, stepped to the woman, and said, "Hello, Beautiful."

"Hello, Popi," the woman answered.

"Can I talk to you at the table?" Champ asked.

The woman smiles and led the way back to the table she occupied before. Champ walks slightly behind her and watches her right arm closely. She sits down and takes a sip of her drink, as she lifts her glass in her right hand, her diamond bracelet rolls backwards and the tattoo is revealed. Champ is excited, just when he thought he was out of the game, a beautiful woman came to assist him. He spoke first. "What's your name?"

The woman smiled. "You know my name." She held out her right arm for him to see the tattoo clearly.

"Yes, I do," he replied.

"What's your name, Popi?" Beautiful asked.

"My name is Champ, and I want to do business with you," he said.

"Of course you do, I remember you from Texas. What do you need me to do?" Beautiful asked. Her real name is Keemi and she was born and raised in the streets of Texas. Her family holds rank as major cocaine distributors of the South. Keemi is a go-getter, a woman driven by loyalty and greed. She firmly subscribes to the code of the streets and sees herself as a businesswoman. Keemi is flashy; she always wears expensive jewelry, drives expensive cars, and brags about being rich. She is untouchable, seductive, and has many men competing for her attention.

Champ is happy that she is beautiful and that she carries herself in a bossy way. He is more interested in unloading the rest of his product and using Keemi to do it. He has no idea that the FBI is building a separate case on Keemi and her role as a drug trafficker. Just when he thought he had caught a break, he actually walked right into the fire.

Chapter 10

Keemi and Champ agree to do business.

"Here is the address," Champ said as he wrote down the information on a small napkin from the bar.

"It's done," Keemi replied and picked up her cell phone to make a call.

"Hey, chica, I need a new washer and dryer delivered to the basement of 1022 Lee Street. I also need a plumber to check under the sink for repairs," Keemi said.

"Yes, where shall I recycle the old appliances?" the female voice asked.

"The washer is about fifty pounds and the dryer is more weight, so take them to the warehouse to be recycled within an hour," Keemi replied.

"It's done," the female voice said and hung up the phone.

"Thanks. Now let me make a call," Champ said as he excused himself from the table. He walked out of the bar and stood outside. The night air was clear and warm. He looked up at the sky and saw the red flashing lights of an airplane flying above. He took out his cell phone and dialed his aunt Layla's number.

"Hello, Ma, it's Champ," he said.

"Hey, baby, what's up?" Layla asked.

"Please go to the house in the morning and leave the basement door unlocked. I'm getting some work done and the plumbers will lock up," he instructed.

"Sure thing, baby. You be safe," Layla said.

"I will. Love you," Champ said.

"I love you too, baby. See you soon," Layla said and hung up the phone. Champ walked back inside and joined Keemi at her table.

"Let's toast to a bright and prosperous future," Champ said as he motioned for the waitress to come over to their table.

"Grey Goose and grapefruit for me and whatever the beautiful lady will have," Champ said.

"I'll have the same," Keemi said to the waitress.

"Coming right up," the waitress replied and walked away to get their drinks.

"So, Beautiful, lovely, sassy lady, who are you here with tonight?" Champ inquired.

"I'm actually on vacation. All work and no play is not for me," Keemi said with a smile.

"Well, now that we are business associates, can I join you?" Champ asked.

"I love a man who is direct and not afraid to ask for exactly what he wants. You may join me and we can celebrate," Keemi replied with a seductive smile.

"I'm very serious about my job and I seem to have found a match in you," Champ said. The waitress returned with their drinks and they both raised their glasses in the air.

"To success and freedom," Keemi said.

"Yes, baby girl, success and freedom," Champ agreed and sipped his drink. Keemi and Champ drank and talked for a few hours before they went upstairs to Keemi's hotel room. They did not have sex that night. Champ lay next to her and held her as they slept.

The next night, the female worker pulls up to 1022 Lee Street under the disguise of a plumber and enters the basement door. She uses a wrench to unscrew the pipe under the sink and pulls out bags of ecstacy pills wrapped in plastic. She secures the pills in the tool box and carries them out of the house. Inside her work truck she secures the pills in the rubber handles of several plungers. She starts the truck and pulls away from the house.

As soon as she leaves, a delivery truck with one white man and one brown-skinned man pull up. They lift the back of their truck and unload a washer and dryer. The safe house is an old house, in need of repair, so the activity doesn't look suspicious.

The two men take the machines inside. The new washer and dryer are really hollow vaults with multiple layers inside. Once inside the house, the delivery men quickly peel off the first layer to unveil an older-looking-model washer and dryer. The men look around and locate the drugs underneath the steps that lead to the first floor of the house. They stuff the inside of the vaults with cocaine and weed, seal the vaults and carry the "older-looking" washer and dryer to the delivery truck.

Keemi set it up so that the delivery truck will return to a warehouse where the drugs will be separated, re-wrapped, and shipped elsewhere. The men will leave the money wrapped inside of several mattresses in a home furniture delivery truck. Champ will profit $400,000 from working with Keemi, and he is grateful. This will be the biggest move that he has ever made and he doesn't have to lift a finger.

After Champ moved the money to a safe place, he focused on Keemi. He is turned on by a woman with power and he wants a taste of that Latino love. Keemi and Champ quickly become a couple. They are discreet, and travel the world together in private jets to secret islands and resorts. He doesn't have to do much with Keemi around. She takes care of everything. She adores him and she does all that she can to keep him satisfied.

Champ pushes Diamond out of his mind. He is good at forgetting the love of a woman since his mother is his best teacher. Keemi makes it easy for him as she insists on all of his attention, all of the time.

Chapter 11

Diamond is off to a strong start at college. She is taking five classes her first semester, and it seems like she lives in the library. Even though Diamond has a computer and work space at home, she likes the library. She is lonely at home, so she surrounds herself with other students, in the library.

Diamond knows that one day she will be called on to do something important, and she wants to be ready. She is engrossed in her class work and as expected, she excels academically. Diamond's advisor notices her intelligence and offers her a part-time job as a clerk in the law library. Diamond doesn't need a job, she has money, but she knows that she will have access to information that won't be available to most students. She accepts the job and works two nights a week.

As a clerk at the law library, Diamond learns how the university information system operates. In addition, she learns how to identify and locate landmark court cases and official documents that deal with all levels of local, state, and federal law.

Most importantly, she has access to the Criminal Justice Information System, a database that collects and stores individual cases both open and closed, at all levels of the criminal justice system. In short, Diamond can type in the name of a person and their entire criminal history, pending criminal charges, and case information are made available. The law library helps to maintain the database for research purposes, but Diamond knows that this database will be an asset someday.

Diamond finishes her freshman year of college with a 3.8 grade point average and a promotion from law library clerk to data entry technician. As a data entry technician, Diamond will work directly with the criminal justice department at the university to enter the most current statistics as reported by the State Justice Department and the FBI. She is excited about her new job, and looks forward to returning to campus in the fall. Diamond wants to go home for a few weeks before summer begins. She schedules two classes for late summer, packs her belongings, and drives home to Valley.

When she arrives home, she is in shock. She knew things would change, but she didn't know exactly how much. Diamond rode down Jackson Street, a main road, and noticed several small stores out of business and boarded up. She was so involved with college work and her job at the library that she neglected to keep in touch with home. She spoke to her mother each week, but Lynne never told her about the changes to the neighborhood.

Diamond made a right turn off of the main road and drove past Champ's old trap house. She didn't see anyone, no corner boys, no dogs, nothing. The grass in the yard is freshly cut, so someone is taking care of the house. Diamond makes another right and drove uptown towards her mother's new house. As she stops at the stop sign she sees Ron, her best male friend from high school. She and Ron lost touch after graduation. Ron attends a football camp out of state and plays quarterback at Penn State University. Ron spots the truck and waves to Diamond. She pulls over and gets out. Ron jogs towards her and picks her up with a big hug and kiss on the cheek.

"Hey, sunshine, I am so happy to see you," Ron exclaimed.

"I missed you too. Where are you headed?" Diamond asked.

"I'm out walking the neighborhood, nowhere really," Ron replied.

"I'm going home; you want to ride with me?" Diamond asked.

"Sure. I thought about you a lot this past year. I knew I would see you again, but I wasn't sure when," Ron said.

"I know we lost touch; I buried myself in my books. It worked out too, because I'm doing really well. Hey, come on, get in the truck so we can roll out," Diamond said. Diamond and Ron got in the truck and she drove up the hill towards home.

"So, did you hear about Rob and Nikki? They got married a few months ago and are having their second child soon. They live in California now," Ron said. He stopped talking and studied Diamond's face for a reaction. She flashed a smile.

"That's good! I'm happy for them. They love each other so they might as well get married," Diamond replied as she drove.

"Sure, sunshine, I'm happy too," Ron said in a sarcastic tone.

Diamond looked at Ron and asked, "What happened to the neighborhood? Businesses are closed and houses are abandoned."

"My mom said that the drugs on the south side dried up and there was a drought in the city, so people started robbing and stealing to survive. Even though drugs are bad, it seems like things got worse once the drugs left. No ballers, no money in circulation. Crime went up and people closed up shop and moved on," Ron replied thoughtfully.

Diamond's mind immediately went to Champ, since he ran the south side. Diamond's brother, Junior, gave up the drug game too. He said the FBI is active in the city and that he doesn't trust anyone anymore. With both Junior and Champ out of the game, the economy is depressed and everyone involved suffers: no dope for the fiends and no money to be made for the hustlers.

Diamond pulls into her mother's driveway and parks the truck. Lynne's car isn't out front. Diamond and Ron go inside. Ron walks to the living room and sits on the couch, while Diamond walks through the house to see if anyone is home. No one is, so Diamond returns to the living room and falls onto the love seat opposite Ron.

"So, did you hear about your man Champ? He hasn't been around lately. I heard from Moe over Christmas break that Champ hooked up with a Spanish dope girl and is on the low out of state," Ron gossiped.

"Oh, really? No, I had not heard about that. It's been a year since I've seen or heard from him. I hope he's safe," Diamond said as her stomach churned at the thought of another woman getting Champ's love and affection.

"Yeah, me too. Anyway, what's in the fridge? I'm hungry," Ron replied and got up to walk to the kitchen.

"Help yourself," Diamond whispered. Her mind wondered. The feelings that she had suppressed for so long came right to the surface and she missed Champ all over again. But she knew the timing was not right for him to be her man. Maybe one day.

Chapter 12

Champ and Keemi are relaxing on a private beach in Florida. Keemi is swimming in the ocean while Champ naps on the sand in a lounge chair. He is dreaming that he is being chased by the police. He runs up a dark alley to get away. Suddenly he wakes up, his heart beats fast and he sits up and looks around. He sees the beach and Keemi in the water swimming. He doesn't move because he knows the dream is a sign. Keemi stops swimming and walks towards him. Champ has to get away from Keemi, he has a bad feeling, and he knows that he has to be alone when it goes down.

Keemi sits in the lounge chair next to him and said, "Hey, love, you sleep well?"

"Not really. How was your swim?" he asked.

"The water is warm and feels wonderful. Do you want to go in with me?" Keemi asked.

"Not right now. Come lay on me," he said and reaches for her. Keemi obeys and lies on top of him.

"What's wrong, baby?" she asked.

"It's time to make a move, Beautiful. I got a feeling that we need to go our separate ways for a little while," Champ said as he looks into her eyes and strokes her wet hair.

"Why, baby? What's wrong?" Keemi asked, confused.

"I care for you, Keemi, and I am grateful for all that you have done for me, but it's time to get out of dodge and we cannot be together during that time," he explained.

She knows he is right. They have been together almost a year now, and she is afraid that if they do get caught, they will be together, and they will both go down. It is better for them to separate so that if one of them gets caught, the other one will be safe and free to help.

Champ said, "In the morning, we will go. You'll fly back alone. We'll keep in touch via phone. If anything happens, hold your own and forget me."

Keemi's eyes swell with tears and she said, "Yes, baby, I understand." Her stomach knots up, and she feels a burning in her throat as she fights to hold back tears. It is no use. She falls on his chest and sobs. The dream team will be separate soon, and Keemi is sad about it. Champ is her equal and her lover. He has heart and is a great businessman. Keemi feels secure in his arms, so she works hard to please him. But all that is about to change, and Keemi is not happy about it.

Keemi lifts her head and looks into Champ's eyes and said, "Baby, I'll do anything for you. I love you, and as long as I live, I'll do what I can to make you happy."

Champ pulls Keemi close and replied, "I love you too, and you will always have a place with me. You are beautiful and powerful, we make a good team. But one day you might have to forget me in order for both of us to be safe. Can you do that for me?"

He leans in to kiss Keemi and she leans in to meet his lips with hers. She sits back and said, "Yes, baby. It will be the hardest thing that I will ever have to do. But to protect you, I will forget you." Keemi looked serious, and Champ knew she meant it.

"Let's spend our last night making love and memories. Tomorrow will have its own worries," Champ said as he begins kissing Keemi's neck and ears. Keemi feels weak; the man of her dreams will soon be gone and she will have to face the world alone.

Chapter 13

The next morning Keemi wakes up to an empty bed. She sits up and looks around for Champ. Keemi smells weed smoke coming from the patio, so she gets out of bed and slips into her robe. Champ is sitting in a chair looking towards the ocean. He hears Keemi approaching. "Good morning, baby. Did you sleep well?"

"Sure did, especially after making sweet love to you," Keemi said with a smile.

"Good. Now get dressed, we have to make that move," he said in a serious tone.

"Oh, baby, just lay with me a little while longer please," Keemi begs.

Champ turns and faces Keemi and said, "Baby, it's time to move. It's a must or else we are at risk for trouble."

Champ didn't sleep at all, in fact, he watched Keemi sleep, and as much as he loves her, he has to let her go. He is uneasy and he knows he has to get away quick.

Keemi steps inside the beach house and gathers her bags. The house belongs to a friend of the family, so she can return whenever she desires. But for some reason Keemi doesn't want to come back, not without Champ, so she quickly packs and gets ready to leave.

Champ gives Keemi specific instructions. "Baby, I'll call you. I'll get a couple burnout phones once I'm safe, so be sure to answer. If anything happens to you, get a message to me through my cousin Moe. I'll stay in touch from time to time. Tell no one about us or where we've been. As far as they know, you have been away on business. Finally, hold your own. The feds want both of us; don't believe anything that they tell you. I love you, and as soon as we are cool, we'll be together again."

Keemi didn't cry this time, she couldn't. She is a boss and she can't be weak right now. Champ pulls her close and kisses her forehead. He leans in and whispers, "Out of sight, out of mind."

Keemi nods her head and watches as he leaves the beach house, gets into the car and drives away. She stands motionless for a moment and asks herself, "Where are you going, Keemi?"

She had connections in almost every state, Canada, and Mexico. Mexico, that's it.

"I'll lay low in Mexico," she said out loud to herself. "At least I'll be close to home and able to make a move if I need to."

But what Keemi doesn't know is that the FBI is patiently waiting to catch her dirty, and that it will only be a matter of time.

Chapter 14

Diamond is enjoying a peaceful summer day at home. Lynne is gardening in the backyard while Diamond sits on the back porch and watches her mother crawl in the dirt. Diamond admires her mother's "green thumb." She asked Lynne, "Do you need any help, Ma?"

"No thanks, baby, I'm almost finished. But you can get me some ice water to drink if you want to be helpful," Lynne replied.

"Sure, Ma," Diamond replied as she gets up to go inside the house. She gets a glass from the wooden cabinet and fills it with ice water. Just as Diamond turns to go back outside the telephone rings.

"Hello," Diamond answered.

"Hi, sunshine. What's up?" Ron asked.

"Not much. Hold on," Diamond put the phone down and took the glass of water to her mother.

"Thanks, baby," Lynne said with a smile.

"You're welcome. I'll be inside," Diamond said as she walks back inside the kitchen and picks up the phone.

"Hello," Diamond said.

"Sunshine, I'm calling to tell you that there's a party on the south side tonight. Will you come?" Ron asked.

"I don't know, whose party?" Diamond asked.

"It's a welcome home party to all those that are home for the summer. There will be a grill, music, and of course a lot of fun," Ron said in an excited tone.

"What time?" Diamond asked.

"Around eight tonight. I'm riding with the fellas, but I'll meet you in front of my house and we will go together," Ron replied.

"Okay, I'll come out for a few hours tonight. I'll see you soon," Diamond confirmed.

"Cool," Ron said and hung up.

Diamond hung up the phone, walked to the screen door, and said, "Ma-ma, I'm going to the nail shop and the mall. Do you need anything?"

"No, baby. Have fun," Lynne replied.

Diamond put on her Baby Phat flip-flops, grabbed her purse, and walked out the door. As she drove to the mall she wondered who might come to the party.

Chapter 15

Diamond is excited. She is dancing as she gets dressed. She pulls the light pink and white tank top over her head and examines herself in the full-length mirror that is on the back of her bedroom door.

"Looking good," she said to herself out loud as she steps into the short, denim jean skirt that she purchased. Diamond finishes the outfit with a light pink belt and pink and white sandals. She applies her lip gloss and make-up to complete her look.

"Mmmmuh," Diamond smiles as she blows a kiss to herself in the mirror. She is ready to go, so she grabs her keys and walks towards the front door.

It is 7:45 p.m., and Diamond is right on time. She hops in her truck and drives to Ron's house on the south side. Ron lives one block north of where Diamond grew up, and they have been close friends since elementary school. As she turns onto Ron's street she can see cars lining both sides. It looks like a block party. Diamond slows down and pulls into Ron's driveway.

Ron is outside and greets Diamond, "Hey, sunshine. Glad you came. Come on in, my mom wants to see you." Diamond gets out of the truck and walks inside.

The living room is occupied by several of the fellas and their lady friends. Diamond speaks as she enters the room, "Hello, everyone."

"Hey, sunshine!" a familiar voice calls back. Diamond takes a few more steps and identifies the familiar voice. It is Rob grinning from ear to ear.

Diamond and Rob used to hang out on and off, for a while, but Rob has a child with Nikki, so the baby momma drama never stops. In the past, Nikki has followed Diamond around town in her car or drove by yelling curse words out the window. Diamond remembers the day that the drama turned to violence and stomping Nikki's head into the pavement.

"Hello, Rob. It's good to see you. Where's mommy at?" Diamond asked.

"I think she's in her room," Rob tells her, smiling. Diamond walks up the steps and down the hall to Lynette's room and knocks.

"Come in," a voice from inside the room calls out. Diamond turns the knob and opens the door.

"Hey, mommy," Diamond said as she enters the room.

"Hey, sugar, I'm so glad to see you. Come in and sit down." Lynette pats on her bed for Diamond to sit down.

"How's college?" Lynette asked.

"I like it so far," Diamond replied.

"Stick with it, baby; you are an intelligent young woman," Lynette said.

"Thank you. How are you?" Diamond asked.

"I'm good, just trying to keep my crazy son focused so he can get out of here one day," Lynette said.

"I know what you mean," Diamond replied.

"Baby, don't let anyone, not even my son, get you off track. You stick to your plan and you will be blessed," Lynette said.

"Thanks, mommy, that really means a lot," Diamond said.

Just then Ron walks into the bedroom and said, "Okay, sunshine, we're ready to go."

"Okay sure," Diamond said and stands to hug Lynette.

"Be safe, baby, and come back to see me," Lynette said.

"I will, and you do the same," Diamond said as she walks out of the bedroom. She follows Ron back downstairs and outside. All of the fellas are outside talking and Rob is leaning on his car staring at Diamond.

Rob looks good to Diamond, but she knows he is a married man with issues. Besides, what they share can never compare to the feelings that Diamond has for Champ.

"Leave your car here; the party is at Moe's house around the corner," Ron said to Diamond.

"Hold up, boo, why didn't you tell me that from the start?" Diamond asks with attitude.

"Because I knew you wouldn't want to come. It's too late now, let's go," Ron said as he grabs Diamond's hand to lead her down the walkway to the sidewalk. She doesn't want to disappoint Ron, so she walks hand in hand with him to the party.

Moe lives exactly two blocks away, and as Diamond gets closer to the house she gets anxious and nervous.

"Please, God, protect me, and get me home safe," she prays.

Ron walks up on Moe's porch and knocks a few times. Moe answers the door and said, "Hey, look what the wind blew in. Come on in, family."

Diamond feels strange entering the house. The furniture is new, and the living room is decorated with scented candles. Moe smiles and nods his head as she walks past him to enter the house.

"The party's out back. Rosa got drinks in the kitchen. The grill man is out back. Make yourselves at home," Moe said as he points in the direction of the party.

Diamond smiles and nods her head as she made her way through the crowd of people in the kitchen drinking. She walks out the back door and outside to join the festivities. The yard is full of people, the music is loud, and the party is definitely in full swing. Diamond finds a lounge chair under the canopy and sits down.

"What am I doing here?" she asked herself. At that moment Rob walks over and asked, "Can I join you?"

Diamond wants to say no, but she doesn't say anything.

"Beautiful night to celebrate," Rob said as he sits down in the chair next to hers.

"Yes, it is nice out tonight," Diamond replied.

"So I hear you're studying to be a lawyer, huh?" Rob asked.

"Yep, you heard right," she said quickly.

"That's excellent. I'm thinking of joining the armed forces myself. I need to learn a skill and travel the world helping people. The money is guaranteed, so I figure I'll make something of myself," Rob announced proudly.

"That's good. You should get out of here and do something positive with your life. You are a good man, you just need room to grow," Diamond said thoughtfully.

"Yes, I'm definitely going to try. Hey, you want to dance?" Rob asked hopefully.

"No, thanks. You go have fun. I'll be right here relaxing," Diamond said.

"Okay, Miss Diamond, I'll see you later," Rob said and gets up to join the party.

Diamond smiles and nods her head. She decides to loosen up and get a drink from the bar in the kitchen. She stands up and walks back through the crowd to the house.

Rosa, Moe's girlfriend, is working the bar. Rosa and Diamond grew up together. They are one year apart. Their mothers hung out when they were little, so they played and fought. They fought more than they played. They attend the same high school, but they are not friends. Rosa pretends to be cool because she is jealous of Diamond.

Rosa is petite and light skinned, with long hair and hazel eyes. She is very pretty and dresses well. Her nickname is "Reds" because she is hot tempered and gets into fistfights often.

Diamond walks up to the bar and said, "Hello, Rosa. Vodka and cranberry please."

"Sure, that will be five dollars," Rosa replied as she quickly stares Diamond up and down. Diamond can sense that Rosa is on the defensive, so she watches very closely as Rosa puts a scoop full of ice into a plastic cup, and pours the alcohol into the cup.

Rosa sets the cup in front of Diamond on the bar. "Hold on while I get your juice," she said.

As Rosa turns to get the cranberry juice from behind her, Diamond put a ten-dollar bill on the counter and said, "No worries, forget the juice. I'm good." She picks up her cup and walks out the back door to the party.

Diamond walks back to her lounge chair under the canopy and sips her drink. The alcohol is strong and she wrinkles her nose as she swallows.

Ron walks over and holds out his hands, "Would you like to dance?" he asked.

Diamond puts the cup to her mouth and quickly swallows the rest of the drink. The alcohol rushes to her head and she relaxes instantly. She is not a drinker, so the alcohol takes immediate effect. Ron holds her hand and leads her to the dance floor.

He treats her with the utmost respect and always makes sure she is comfortable when they are together.

Diamond loves to dance and she feels good swaying her body to the music. She moves effortlessly and looks sexy doing it. Suddenly, Rob bumps Ron out the way. Ron steps back as his best friend moves in to dance with Diamond.

She moves her hips in exotic circles and moves close to him. She stares into Rob's eyes as they move. She spins around and he moves in behind her. He puts his hands on her waist and their bodies move together to the music.

Her body catches fire, and memories of lovemaking flood her mind. She dances harder, grinding her body against his. Rob whispers in her ear, "I miss you, sunshine. You are still the most beautiful girl I know."

Diamond smiles and knows that he still lusts for her. But she is no fool, tipsy and all. She turns around to face Rob and said, "Baby, we can have wonderful sex tonight and reminisce. But tomorrow it won't mean a thing. Go home to your wife; she'll get you right, I'm sure."

Rob looks shocked and Diamond smiles at him as she walks away, leaving him standing there. She feels empowered as she walks back into the house.

The kitchen is busy; there is a line of people at the bar. Diamond makes her way through the crowd and walks to the living room. The steps to get to the second-floor bathroom are behind the front door. Moe is still working the door and sees her coming his way.

"Where are you going?" he asked.

"To the bathroom, sir," Diamond responded as she walks past him up the steps.

"Do you remember where it is?" Moe asked, watching as she walks up the steps.

"I got it, thanks," she replied without looking back.

Inside the bathroom she takes a deep breath and relieves herself. She washes her hands and checks herself in the mirror. She is ready to go home; one drink had her loose, and she doesn't need any trouble.

She puts on some lip gloss and pops a piece of gum into her mouth. She straightens her back and shoulders as she walks back downstairs, past Moe, and out the front door. She walks briskly down the front steps and two blocks to her truck. She gets inside and locks the doors. She adjusts her seat back and closes her eyes. She can't drive, so she takes a nap.

Chapter 16

It is 2:00 a.m. and Diamond opens her eyes. She has been asleep for hours. She starts her truck and pulls out of Ron's garage. She drives past Moe's party and it is still going strong. She drives straight, two more blocks past Champ's old trap house: there are lights on in the basement. She turns left and drives past the side of the house. She notices movement in the basement.

"I wonder who that is?" Diamond asked herself.

Being a pre-law student and naturally inquisitive, she circles the block and parks out of sight to investigate. She has a good view of the house and can clearly see movement in the basement. She lays her seat back and watches to see who will come out of the house.

So many questions are running through her mind: "Who is creeping late at night at Champ's trap?" "And what are they doing inside?" "If it is him, what am I going to do?"

The basement light goes out and a person emerges from the back gate. She can't see who it is because the person has a black hoodie pulled over his head, black pants, and all-black sneakers. Diamond watches as the mystery person carries two black duffle bags into the alley.

Diamond lost view, but she doesn't move. She is caught up in the moment. She has to find out who is in the car, but she is a little afraid. She could be witnessing a transaction of some kind, and she doesn't want to interrupt.

The navy blue Lincoln eases out of the alley and drives directly towards Diamond. She gets low in the seat and lets the car pass. She watches in her mirror to see what direction the car will turn. It makes a left and Diamond quickly starts her car to follow.

The south side is busy at night. The young people party and bar-hop, while the dope fiends and drug addicts walk the streets looking for a hit. The young, fast girls walk up and down the block in their short shorts and tube tops, trying to get the attention of the men and hustlers.

Diamond tries to keep up with the Lincoln, but she can't. The driver of the Lincoln speeds up and starts making quick left and right turns down dark, back roads. Diamond doesn't want to risk her safety, so she backs off, stops following the Lincoln, and drives home.

She pulls in front of her mother's house, turns off the truck, and unlocks the doors to get out. Just as she opens her door and steps out, a dark-colored car speeds down the street. It is the Lincoln.

Diamond pulls her body inside the truck and prays, "Lord protect me and guide me, Amen."

The Lincoln circles the block and turns out the headlights as it approaches the truck. The car pulls beside Diamond's truck and the window rolls down slow. Diamond's heart drops and her stomach flips.

"So are you following me now?" Champ asked with a smile.

Diamond doesn't hear him, she's afraid to sit up far enough to see him. He takes his hood off and speaks louder, "You getting bold these days, huh, Diamond?"

She sits up slowly and realizes that it's him. She rolls down her window and stares at him.

"Listen, I was going to make a move, but now that I've seen you, I changed my mind. I got two bags off old cash that I need to be kept safe and I trust you. Will you take them inside?" Champ asked.

Diamond is in shock. This is unreal, not only did the love of her life just pop up, but he's asking for a huge favor on top of it.

"Listen, Diamond, I have to go. If you take the bags I have a reason to find you and come back," Champ stated.

Diamond finally spoke. "I'll hold you down, but I'm leaving in a few weeks for summer classes. If you are not back, I'll leave them here."

"That's why I love you. My queen, no questions asked. I'll pull into the alley," Champ said.

"I'll meet you out back," Diamond said.

She gets out of the truck and sprints up the front steps to open the door. She is careful moving through the house in the dark.

Champ is standing on the back porch with the bags when Diamond gets there. She opens the back door and lets him in.

He looks handsome, but very tired. His eyes have dark circles underneath them, and his eyes are low and red.

"You can take the bags to the basement. Junior got a secret spot," Diamond whispered. Champ walks towards the basement door, when Diamond grabs his arm.

"I'm so happy that you are safe," she said.

"Thanks, baby. I'm glad to see you too. Now show me the way," Champ said.

Diamond opens the basement door and turns on the light. She leads the way downstairs. The basement is finished, so there is a carpeted area with furniture and a television. There is a washing area with a large sink, a washer and dryer, and a small office area. The bathroom is the secret spot. It is for show because the walls of the bathtub and shower flip inside out to reveal secret compartments.

Diamond pushes a tiny switch under the shower head and the bottom of the tub rises up and rolls over to provide a space large enough to hold both black bags.

Champ quickly places the bags into the spaces and secures them with the straps inside the space. Diamond hits the switch again and the tub floor returned to its place.

She turns to face Champ and said, "I'm leaving in two weeks to go back to school. Let me write down my address and phone numbers for you so that can reach me."

She quickly moves to the coffee table and bends down to use

the ink pen and pad. She scribbles her information for him. As she is writing, he stands directly behind her. When she stands up and turns to give him the paper, he is directly in front of her, face to face.

"Diamond, you are my savior and one day you are going to be my wife," Champ said while looking into her eyes.

"Here, baby, take this. Finish your business and catch up with me when you are ready to relax. It's been a while and I miss you," Diamond said as she put the piece of paper in his hand.

He takes the paper and follows Diamond up the steps and out the back door.

"Be safe. I love you," Diamond said as he walks back to his car.

"I'll see you soon, baby girl," Champ said as he gets into the car.

Diamond stands still to process in her mind all that just happened. He pulls off, and she walks back inside the house. She sets the burglar alarm, checks the locks on the doors, and walks upstairs to her room.

Inside her room she takes off all of her clothes and crawls into bed. She is exhausted and in a daze. After a whole year of no contact, she sees her love again. Not only did she see him, but she touched him and smelled his scent. She accepted money from him; she is now directly tied to him. She is excited, and the thought of him and another woman fueled her fire. She knows Champ is her man.

Chapter 17

Champ has so many moves to make and little time to do it. He isn't sure how much information the FBI has gathered so he wants to clean off all the property that he is associated with, as well as move all of his money to safekeeping. His logic is that selling the properties that he owns will look suspicious, so he will find a person to manage the properties as rentals. A portion of the money collected from rent will go into a business account for profit, and the remaining money will be used to pay the manager's salary and maintenance for the property.

The properties were purchased by Moe's mother, Layla. Auntie Layla has a good-paying job as a registered nurse at a private residential facility. The cost of land and housing in Valley is cheap, so Layla can afford to own several properties. Champ can trust Auntie Layla to remodel and maintain the properties, as well as, direct the funds accordingly. He follows his gut and calls his aunt.

"Hello," Layla answered her cell phone.

"Hey, Mommy, it's Nephew," Champ said.

"Hi, baby. How are you?" Layla asked happily.

"Better when I see you; will you meet me for dinner at the house?" he asked.

"Sure, baby. Is 10:00 p.m. okay?" she asked.

"I love you. See you soon," he said and hung up the phone. He has a few hours before then, so he decides to relax and contemplate his next move.

"Where am I going?" "What exactly am I running from?" "How's Keemi doing?" "What is Diamond thinking?" "How am I going to secure my money and get it into circulation at the same time?" Champ has so many questions that need answered.

He can't be still, he has too much on his mind. He grabs his motorcycle keys and helmet and takes a ride.

The solitude of the dark back roads is peaceful. Champ drives to a large lake about a mile from the house that Auntie Layla will meet him at. The lake is dark and the sound of the crickets is relaxing to Champ. He walks around the lake and takes deep breaths of the night air. He rolls his head from side to side and releases the stress.

He has to think clearly if he is to get out of the game safely. He walks back to his motorcycle and drives to meet his aunt at the house. The house is the same house that Keemi's people removed the drugs from. This house has hidden passageways and safes hidden in the wall.

As he pulls into the driveway, he notices the lights on inside, but Layla's truck isn't out front. He parks his bike and walks around the back of the house. Her truck is out back and she is inside. He calls her cell phone.

"Hello," she answered.

"Hi, Mommy. I'm out back," Champ said.

"Okay, be right there," she assured him. Layla opens the basement door and Champ walks inside.

She immediately hugs her nephew and kisses his cheek. "Happy to see you, baby. Now what's up?"

"I'm laying low indefinitely and I won't be around to keep up with the properties. I want to ask for your help," Champ stated.

"Well, what's the plan?" Layla asked.

"I would like to rent out each house for the next couple years and collect rent money. A small portion will be deposited into an account, while the remaining funds are used to pay your salary and maintenance," Champ explained. "After a few years, you can sell them, but for now let's hold on to them and build a little savings," he continued.

"Well, baby, I am a busy woman and you are asking a lot of me, but I'll do it. I would love to renovate and decorate the properties," Layla replied.

"Good, you already have keys to each house. They are all clean. Thank you, Mommy," Champ said.

"You're welcome. Stay in touch, baby," Layla said.

"I will," Champ answered as he gave his aunt a hug and kiss.

"I got to go, baby. Be safe," Layla said as she walked out the basement door to her car and got inside. Champ turns off the basement light and pulls the door shut behind him. He gets on his bike and rides out.

Chapter 18

Champ drives his bike to Diamond's house, her truck is out front and her bedroom light is on. He revs the engine twice and waits. She is inside her room listening to music when she hears the noise.

He pulls off and circles the block. As she opens her bedroom door to walk to the front door, she can hear a motorcycle coming up the block. She walks outside and sees Champ slowing down in front of her house. He stops and signals for her to come to him.

Diamond is happy to go, and she walks towards him to find out what he needs. He didn't take his helmet off, but flips the top portion up to reveal his eyes.

She stood on the curb in front of her house and asked, "Yes, love, how can I help you?"

"Will you ride with me?" he asked.

"Where to and for how long?" she replied.

Champ smirked and said, "Someplace far and for the night."

"Meet me out back in a few minutes; I have to grab a few things," Diamond said.

He nods and pulls off. She walks back inside and gathers her things: a black book bag, a toothbrush, soap, lotion, a hair brush, two pairs of shorts, panties, and two t-shirts. She walks towards the back door and grabs her keys and purse. She stops at a small table and scribbles a note to her mother before she leaves.

Champ is waiting in the alley and he asked, "Do you still have your helmet?"

"Yes. Let me get it," she replied. Diamond walks to a small tool shed to get the helmet. She quickly secures the book bag on her back, pulls the helmet on her head, and climbs on the back of the motorcycle. She holds Champ tight as he revs the engine and pulls off into the night.

She watches as everything moves by fast. He rides down the highway towards the private airport that he uses for business. He always has a plane ready and waiting.

He owns a large, black cargo plane that he is trained to fly. It is all black inside and out and has six seats and plenty of cargo space for business and travel.

He pulls into the entrance to the airport and enters his gate code to get inside. The gate rolls open and he quickly drives inside. He drives straight to the runway parking lot where his plane is parked and secured.

Diamond has done this before, exactly one year before. The summer that she graduated from high school was full of trips and excitement. He spoiled her, and bought her jewelry and gifts. He dressed and undressed her. They spent almost every day together before she went off to college. Now she is in his arms again, and she wants to be with him.

The cargo plane is backed into a giant garage. Champ pulls in and parks the motorcycle. He turns towards Diamond to help her off of the bike. They stand face to face and he stares deep into her eyes. He puts his arms around her waist and pulls her close to him. She can feel her blood rushing to her face as her cheeks turn rosy.

"I get butterflies every time you touch me," Diamond admitted.

"I love touching you. I've been missing you," Champ said as he leans in to kiss her lips. Her knees get weak as she returns the passion and kisses him.

"Come on, let's go. I have a wonderful surprise for you," he said when the kiss ended.

He secures his motorcycle in the garage and helps Diamond into the plane. She watches him as he walks around the front of the plane to get into the pilot's seat. As soon as he gets inside, she crawls over the gears that separate them and straddles him. She is in heat and she wants him bad.

She kisses him, a slow tongue kiss. She licks his neck and kisses his ears. The pilot's seat is a small area so their bodies are pressed close. She stops kissing him and puts both of her hands on his face.

She looks directly into his eyes and said, "Baby, I'm in love with you. And even though you've been away, my feelings for you have grown stronger every day. I am focused on school and my future, but I can't shake the feeling of wanting to be with you forever."

"Diamond, let me take you somewhere special and you can show me just how much you care," he said with a smile.

"Okay," she said and kisses his forehead. She moves back across the gears to her seat and positions herself for take off.

"Put on your headset, baby. You are my copilot; you have to always know what's going on," Champ said. Diamond adjusts her headset and put it on while he flips switches and starts the plane.

"We are flying with the stars tonight," he said. The plane begins to roll forward and Diamond takes a deep breath.

"Are you ready, baby?" Champ asked.

"Yes, daddy, let's go," she replied.

The plane rolls onto the runway and gains speed.

"Enjoy this moment, baby; it's meant for us to fly high together," Champ said as the plane picks up speed for takeoff.

Diamond is anxious because loving him is like a double-edged sword. On one hand he is a successful businessman. He is fair and reliable, as well as efficient. He travels alone and never forces his hustle. On the other hand, he is a vicious dope dealer that manages a tight drug network. He has a dark, violent side that sometimes calls for murder. Diamond doesn't want to get mixed up in any of his transactions, nor does she want to be a co-conspirator on any of his charges.

Champ flew the plane high above the ground and she watches as the houses disappeared below. She enjoys looking down at the city night lights. It is beautiful and peaceful in the sky and she feels a calm come over her.

"May I ask where we're going?" Diamond said in the headset.

"To Canada for a few days. My cousin lives there and I want you to meet him," Champ said.

"Baby, I trust you, but how can you just fly right into Canada without being detected or cause trouble?" Diamond asked.

Champ chuckled, "We can because my cousin owns the airport that I'm flying to. All we have to do is call him and get clearance to land. Watch this," Champ said, dialing a number on the telephone pad on the dashboard. Diamond can hear the number dialing and a ringing sound in her headset.

"Good evening, this is control tower 304. How may I help you?" a male voice asked.

"Control tower 304, this is Night Bird calling, do I have clearance for landing?" Champ asked in serious tone.

"Night Bird all clear to land," the voice replied.

"Copy 304, en route," Champ responded. He flew the plane north for about two hours. Diamond is silent during the flight. Champ re-dials the number and waits for someone to pick up.

"Good evening, this is control tower 304. How may I help you?" a man's voice asked.

"Control tower 304, this is Night Bird ready to land," Champ said.

"Night Bird all clear," the voice responded.

Champ slowly circles a small, private airport with white lights flashing. He lowers the plane and steadies the wheel. He put the plane's wheels down and lands the plane. Diamond's ears pop and her body jerks back and forth as the plane's wheels hit the ground and it rolls forward on the runway. Champ pumps the breaks and brings the plane to a halt. He takes off his headset and smiles at Diamond.

"Thanks for the ride," she said with a smile.

"We're in Canada, baby. Come on, let's go meet my cousin," Champ said as he opens the pilot's door and gets down from the plane. Diamond grabs her backpack and gets off the plane. Champ walks around the plane, takes Diamond's hand, and leads her off the runway towards the control tower.

A tall, dark-skinned man exits the control tower to greet them. As he approaches, Diamond examines him from head to toe. He is well over six feet tall, with a medium build. He has a low haircut and light brown eyes. He is very attractive and walks with confidence. He wears a huge smile on his face, with gold and diamond teeth. Champ picks up his pace and walks happily towards his cousin. The men meet with a special handshake. The kind of handshake where two men pull each other in towards one another in a semi-hug, a greeting reserved for close friends and loved ones.

"Baby, meet Davion, my cousin on my father's side," Champ said as he grabs Diamond by her hand, pulling her in front of him, and putting his arms around her.

"Hello, nice to meet you," Diamond responds with a smile and extends her hand to shake his. Davion steps forward and accepts her hand. But rather than shake it, he kisses her hand.

"Beautiful, Cousin. What's your name, family?" Davion asked.

"Diamond." She blushed.

"Okay, Cousin, I'll kill for this one. So what's good with you?" Champ asked.

Davion motions for them to come inside. Diamond and Champ follow him past the control tower entrance to a second door and walk inside.

She is amazed at what she sees. A huge, high-tech efficiency apartment with a living room full of black leather furniture; a queen-sized bed with black satin sheets; a large flat-screen TV; a computer; and a kitchen area.

"Welcome to the lab, family. Nothing but black love in here. Make yourselves at home," Davion said with a smile. He walks towards the fridge and pulls out two beers and bottled water.

Diamond walks over to get the bottled water and said, "Thanks."

She walks over to the couch and sits on the love seat and quietly exhales. She is living a dream, and once again Champ is responsible for taking her places and showing her things.

"Ya'll want to go to the falls tomorrow?" Davion asked as he sips his beer.

"Do you mean Niagara Falls?" Diamond asked.

"Yes, the falls are a sight to see, especially at night," Davion said.

Diamond smiles and shakes her head in approval of the idea.

"Baby, I'm going talk to Davion outside for a few minutes. Will you make yourself comfortable? We're going to rest here for the night? Get ready for me, baby; when I come back in, I'll want you to show me how much you love me," Champ said as he sits down next to Diamond on the love seat.

She smiles and kisses his lips.

"I got you, daddy. See you in a few," Diamond said.

Davion grabs both beers off the counter, waves good-bye to Diamond, and walks out of the door. Champ follows Davion to the control tower and takes a seat next to him. In front of them is a giant computer screen with buttons, flashing lights, and green radar screens.

Chapter 19

Champ and Davion purchased land in Canada and set up greenhouses to grow cannabis under the Canadian Industrial Hemp laws. The difference between the bud Champ smoked every day and the cannabis that is legal to grow in Canada is the THC content of the plants. Cannabis that has hardly any THC content can be grown and used to create thousands of products including clothing, paper, oil, food products, and more. The bud that Champ smokes has high THC content and is grown specifically for getting high.

Davion majored in biology in college and minored in business. He always knew that he wanted to grow bud legally, and hemp is as close as he can get. The land that they purchased was twenty acres of farmland about four miles from the private airport that Davion owned. Business was booming and Champ saw hundreds of thousands of dollars in profit and return. Champ owned a farmhouse of his own that he planned to retire to one day.

Champ takes a sip of his beer and said, "I have to leave the states soon, Cousin. The feds got one of my folks, and I need to lay low for a few."

"Well, Cousin, you know you got a house here. You and baby girl can relocate and chill out for a while," Davion replied.

"I'm going to talk to Diamond tonight and see what she thinks. I got enough money from your work here put away, and the funds that I've made in the states should be enough to retire with," Champ said as he sips his beer. He raises his bottle in the air. "Let's toast to the future as farmers."

"No doubt, there's a constant need and a wide open economy for growing hemp here in Canada; the states are way behind on this. Yeah, Cousin, it's time to move up and move on," Davion replied and carefully clashes his bottle against Champ's.

The sky is clear and the air was warm. The two men finish their beer and leave the tower. On the way back to the apartment Champ enjoys a blunt in solitude. He inhales deep and holds the smoke in for a long time. He exhales and lifts his head to the sky.

As a boy, Champ was raised in the church so he knew that God was real, and for the first time in a long time a calm came over him as he knocked on the door of the apartment where Diamond was. She opened the door and smiled as Champ walked in.

"Welcome home, daddy. I missed you," she said.

"Oh, yeah? Show me, baby, just how much you missed me," he said. Diamond leads him to the couch and just before he sits down she unzips his jeans and pulls them down. He steps out of the fallen shorts and takes off his boxers. He sits down on the black sheet that Diamond has spread out on the couch in anticipation of what will happen next.

She stands in front of him, leans over, and pulls his t-shirt off. He is now sitting naked with manhood at attention like a soldier saluting his lieutenant. Diamond dances slowly as she takes off each piece of her clothing. She looks at him with desire in her eyes; she teases him and dances exotically in front of him.

She gets on her knees and kisses his thighs. She licks his stomach and bites his chest. She straddles him and kisses his neck and ears. Champ moans and gets hotter with each touch. Diamond slides down his body and licks her soldier like a chocolate ice cream cone on a hot summer day. She sucks him and grabs him. His head falls back against the couch and his eyes roll back in his head.

He ran his fingers through her long black hair and whispered, "That's it, baby, get daddy."

She gets up, kisses his lips and said, "I love tasting you, baby."

Diamond mounts Champ and rides him thoroughly, grinding her body against his. Champ returns the passion and kisses her breasts and rubs her back. Diamond arches her back and begins to move faster.

"Slow down, baby," Champ said. She ignores his request, and continues to ride him. Her body catches fire and she presses down hard on him. He can feel her climaxing and squeezing inside. He can't hold back and he too climaxes as she continues to move on top of him. Their breathing is hard and their heart rates are up. She gets up and falls across him onto the couch to rest.

"Thanks, baby girl. You know you got me don't you?" Champ asked with his eyes closed.

"You're welcome, daddy. I know you love me," Diamond replied without lifting her head to look at him.

Champ takes a deep breath, stands up, leans over, and picks Diamond up. He walks slowly to the bed and gently laid her down.

He lies beside her and looks into her eyes and said, "Baby girl, you are my number one woman. I trust you. I know you have worked hard in school, and that you have hopes and dreams of your own. I want to ask you to make a place for me in your life."

She runs her fingers down the side of his face and smiled, "Daddy, what exactly are you saying?"

He takes a deep breath and said, "Baby, I've worked hard to get what I have: money, property, a plane, all the material possessions a man could ask for and more. While working I've drawn the attention of the FBI and I have to stay here in Canada for a while. I want you to stay with me."

Her stomach knotted up and her throat went dry. She is flattered, but all she can hear in her head was her brother's voice saying, "Stay focused. Never let a man sell you his dreams and steal yours. You are your own woman, not a foolish man's wife."

Diamond blinks and stops rubbing his face. She sits up in the bed, takes a deep breath and said, "Daddy, I love you. You are gentle and sweet. You keep me safe and please my body. But, baby, I do have my own dreams, and I am in school, and I cannot

risk my future and the sacrifice of my mother and brother to run away with you."

Champ sits up next to her, takes her hands, and replied, "I would never sacrifice your freedom or safety. I understand your position. Keep that money that's at your house and make it multiply the best way you know how. I know you have a bright future ahead of you and I only want to be a part of it."

"Thanks, daddy. Let's enjoy being here together right now," Diamond said as she leans over to kiss him.

He stops her and said, "Baby girl, you are a winner and I won't let you go."

He pulls her close and holds her. She kisses him and put her head on his chest. She listened to his heartbeat until she fell asleep.

The next morning Champ woke up before Diamond. He lay still next to her and watched her sleep. Diamond woke up and rubbed her eyes.

"Good morning, love," she said.

"Good morning," Champ replied.

"Are we going to see the falls today?" she asked.

"Yes, but I want to show you the farms first. I have a retirement plan here and I want you to see it," Champ said.

"Okay, so what's for breakfast?" Diamond asked as she walks her naked body to the refrigerator. She opens the door and found fresh fruit inside: apples, oranges, and grapes. She found bottled water and beer to drink.

"Looks like Davion eats healthy. Are you hungry, baby?" Diamond asked.

"No, thanks, baby; you enjoy. I'll take some cold water though," Champ replied.

Diamond grabs an orange and two bottled waters and walks back to the bed.

"Thank God for today, daddy. I feel good," Diamond said as she peels her orange and sips her water.

"Good, baby, I'm glad you're happy. I'm going to shower while you eat," Champ said.

He walks his naked body across the apartment to the shower and went inside. Diamond remains on the bed eating her orange and thinking about what life with Champ as her husband will be like.

Just as she finished her orange, Champ yells from inside the shower, "Baby, come here for a minute please."

"Yes, love, coming," she replied. Diamond grabs her book bag and went to the bathroom. It is steamy and hot inside. She gets her toothbrush from her bag and brushes her teeth.

Champ pulls the shower curtain back and said, "Will you get in with me? I want to wash your body."

Diamond nods her head and quickly rinses her mouth. She gets in the shower behind him. The water is warm and steady. Champ puts soap on a rag and washes her body. She closes her eyes and relaxes. She imagines being his wife and having his baby. She envisions a life of happiness and safety.

"Okay, baby, you're all clean. I'm going to get out while you rinse off," Champ said.

"Thank you, daddy. You are working hard to please me and I appreciate you," Diamond said.

Champ kisses her, gets out of the shower, and leaves the bathroom. Diamond stands under the warm water and puts her face directly in the water. She washes her hair and lets the water run down her back. She gets out of the shower and wraps her hair up in a towel. As Diamond exits the bathroom, she smells blueberries, the fragrance of Champ's blunt.

"Early morning med call, huh?" she joked.

Champ looks at her and nods. Suddenly there is a knock at the door. Diamond is startled and runs to the bathroom.

Champ asked loudly, "Yeah?"

"It's me, D. Ya'll ready to go?" Davion asked.

Champ is dressed and walks outside to greet Davion. Inside the bathroom, Diamond puts on the shorts and t-shirt that she packed. Her hair is wet and curly. She dries it with the towel, brushes it, and shakes her hair to let it fall into place.

When Diamond walks outside, Davion greets her with a smile, "Good morning, Diamond. Did you sleep well?"

"Yes, thank you," Diamond replied.

"Are you ready to see the land today?" Davion asked.

"Ready when you are," she replied.

Davion walks towards a black SUV; Champ and Diamond follow. They drive a few miles down a long, secluded farm road. On both sides of the road are cannabis plants at least four feet tall.

"Wow, is that bud growing?" Diamond asked.

"Not bud, cousin, hemp. It's the same plant as bud, but you can't get high because the THC content of the plant is very low. These plants are grown and sold to fashion designers and the textile industry to make clothing and fabrics, as well as to builders and bakers to make housing materials and baked goods. This plant is versatile and in high demand worldwide because each part of the plant can be used for a different purpose," Davion informed her.

"So it's bud, but you don't smoke it? You sell it to people to make clothing products? What happened to good old cotton?" Diamond asked curiously.

"Hemp is stronger and longer lasting than cotton. Hemp is used for many more products, like rope and canvas; even the seeds can be used for oil. This plant has 25,000 known uses; cotton cannot compete!" Davion said.

"Is this all your land?" Diamond asked.

"This is my entire land, sweetheart. I'm taking you to your man's land; he has about ten acres of hemp growing. Of course I manage his crops and do all the work, and he collects profits without even lifting a finger," Davion said.

"Watch it, cousin, I'm the silent partner. I do my thing and you do yours," Champ said.

"It's all love, family. You know I'm just messing with you," Davion replied playfully.

The SUV makes a left onto a hidden driveway and a large white house comes into view. As they get closer, Diamond can see hemp growing in the background. It looks like it stretches for miles behind the house. The SUV stops and they get out. Diamond has never seen anything like this. It reminds her of pictures in her black history books of the old southern plantations in the states. A big white house surrounded by acres of crops as far as she could see.

Champ and Diamond follow Davion inside. The house is huge and barely furnished. Diamond is in awe as she walks through the house. Upstairs are four large bedrooms, two of them empty. All of the windows have blinds and curtains, but she can tell by the smell of each room that no one lives here.

She walks downstairs and onto the back porch. In the yard is a storage shed. She walks through the yard to the hemp fields. She is totally amazed. A plant that is criminalized in the states is grown commercially in Canada. She is standing between rows of cannabis and she feels excited.

She wonders exactly what kinds of products are made and who they are sold to. She wonders if there was a market for hemp products in the states, and then it dawns on her: a head shop. A small novelty store on campus that sells t-shirts made of hemp specially designed with catchy phrases; hemp bracelets and jewelry; candles; purses; and backpacks. Diamond is daydreaming when she hears footsteps approaching.

"Hey, baby girl, are you ready to see the falls?" Champ asked.

"Sure, daddy, let's go," she replied.

Champ takes her hand and leads her towards the house. Davion is already waiting in the truck when they exit the house.

"So what do you think, Diamond?" Davion asked when she gets in the truck.

"Very interesting," she said.

Her mind is moving fast; she is processing all that she just saw.

Davion takes the same roads back towards the airport. She looks out the window and daydreams. She thinks about all the possible locations on campus to start a small head shop where students can shop and relax. She imagines signing the deed to the property and becoming a small business owner. She thinks about taking real estate law courses and tax law courses next semester.

"This is the tourist district. The falls are just past these hotels," Davion said, interrupting her thoughts. He drives a few more miles and parks in front of a huge guardrail that runs the full length of the street.

"Let's park here and walk. You get a full appreciation for the falls if you walk next to them," Davion said with a smile.

As soon as Diamond gets out of the truck she can hear the loud sound of rushing water and she can feel the mist of the falls in the air. Champ walks beside her as she follows Davion to the entrance.

It is an amazing sight to see, Niagara Falls. The water rushes quickly down into a huge body of water below. A tourist steamship navigates the waters below while the people on board wear yellow or white rain coats. The mist is cool as it rises in all directions. Diamond is excited; she feels like a little girl, happy and smiling.

She turns to Champ and said, "Baby, you are the best man God has ever blessed me with. You make me feel special when you take me places and show me things."

"I want to make you happy, baby girl," he replied.

Diamond stands behind Champ and puts her arms around his

waist. She closes her eyes and prays silently, "God, thank you for today. Thank you for showing me your wonderful majesty. Please speak to me and guide me. Amen." When Diamond opens her eyes she sees a rainbow arching over the falls, she takes it as a sign to follow her heart.

"Baby, I will stay with you. But I have to finish school first. I promise to be with only you, but I won't be happy unless I finish school and show proper respect to my family."

"I will wait for you, Diamond. I told you, I'm not letting you go," Champ assured her. She smiles and he kisses her and holds her close.

Chapter 20

Champ flew Diamond home the next night. As he is landing the plane he notices two black SUV trucks at the end of the runway. He lands the plane but does not get out. He watches nervously as the two middle-aged white men get into the trucks and pull off. Champ parks the plane and helps Diamond out.

"Baby, I have a strange feeling. When I take you home, stay inside until you leave to go back to college. No malls or parties, okay," Champ said in a serious tone.

Diamond already knows his feeling and she agrees.

"Sure, I can relax until I leave," Diamond assured him. Just then, his cell phone vibrated on his hip and he answered it, "Hello."

"Yeah, it's me, Cousin. Mommy is sick, the ambulance just took her to the hospital. Can you meet me there?" the voice on the phone said.

"Which hospital is she going to?" Champ asked.

"Providence on the north side," the caller's voice yelled.

"On my way," he said as he hung up his cell phone and looked at Diamond sadly.

"What is it, daddy?" Diamond asked.

"It's my auntie, Moe's mom, she's in the ambulance on the way to the hospital," Champ responded.

"Let's go," Diamond said.

She grabs his hand and ran towards the motorcycle parked in the garage. Champ runs with her, hops on his bike, and speeds off to Diamond's house. Diamond jumps off the bike when they pull up in front of her house, kisses his helmet and said, "I love you, baby. Get to the hospital and be safe."

Champ nods his head and speeds off into the night.

At the hospital, Moe paces the hallways while his mother is being treated. Champ calls his cell phone to ask, "What floor, Cousin?"

"Emergency, she's being treated for severe stomach pains," Moe replied, almost crying.

"Got it," Champ said and hung up. When he walks through the emergency room doors and sees Moe's facial expression, he knows it's serious.

Champ stands outside the door of the room where his aunt is being treated. The first nurse to exit the room is a young, white woman with blond hair and blue eyes.

"Excuse me, miss, that's my mother in there. Can you tell me what is going on?" he asked.

"Yes, your mom has a large stomach ulcer that ruptured. She is in severe pain and has some internal bleeding," the nurse said.

"What will you do to fix the problem?" Champ asked.

"She is being prepped for emergency surgery; we must stop the bleeding and remove all parts of the ulcer right away. Now excuse me, I have to call upstairs to let them know that she is on her way," the nurse said and walks quickly to the phone on the wall a few feet away.

Champ's head drops low. His world is turning upside down. The pressure of the feds and now this; it is too much to handle at one time. Moe slides down the wall and sits on the floor. Champ sits down next to him. They say nothing to each other and wait until the door opens and Layla is rolled out on a hospital bed yelling and moaning.

They follow her to the elevator and remain silent as they witness her in pain. When the elevator door opens, the nurses quickly roll Layla inside. Champ and Moe board too. The elevator stops on the third floor and the doors open. The surgical team is standing outside the door to intercept. Layla is rolled swiftly through the gray double doors, into the operating room.

Moe and Champ pace the waiting area for two hours, before the same nurse came back and spoke to them.

"Your mother is stable. She will be in the intensive care unit tonight. She is unconscious right now, but you can see her for a few minutes before she goes upstairs," the nurse reported.

Moe and Champ both nod, and Champ said, "Lead the way please."

The nurse turns and leads them through the double doors and into a small washroom.

"You must wash from the elbows down. She cannot hear you because she is heavily sedated," the nurse instructed.

Moe and Champ did as the nurse requested and walk slowly into the room where Layla is hooked to an IV, a heart monitor, and an oxygen mask on her face. Champ walks to her bedside and holds her hand. He stares at his aunt and his emotions take over. Both Champ and Moe sob loudly as they touch her hands, arms, and forehead.

"Please, God, take care of my mom," Moe prayed out loud.

The nurse re-enters the room and said, "She will recover. We just have to watch her closely overnight for infection and to make sure she doesn't bleed anymore. The ulcers were removed, so she should feel better soon."

"Can I stay with her?" Moe asked.

"Yes, she will be in room 530 on the fifth floor. You can meet me up there," the nurse replied.

Champ leans over, kisses Layla, and whispers, "Hold on, Mommy. We love you here."

"Okay, gentlemen, I'm going to ask you two to meet me upstairs," the nurse said.

Moe and Champ walk out of the room, back through the wash area, and through the double doors.

"I got to go, Cousin. You stay with her. I'll be back in the morning," Champ said to Moe. Moe said nothing. He nods his head and walks towards the elevator. Champ follows him to the elevator and watches him get on and go up. When the next elevator came, Champ went down to the first floor and left the hospital.

Chapter 21

As Champ steps into the cool night air, he is tense, hungry, and seriously agitated. He calls his money man to let him know what is going on.

"Yeah," a man's voice answered.

"It's Champ. Momma's sick, and the alphabet boys were on the runway today," he replied.

"I'm hip. I'm about to clean house tonight and lay low. Do you want to ride?" the man asked.

"Last time and it's done, right?" Champ asked.

"Meet the team at Lil Man's house. It's all in motion," the man said and hung up the phone.

Champ secures his cell phone on his hip and walks slowly to his motorcycle. His mind is on overload; and he has to be very careful.

Valley is a border city and is located ten miles from the Pennsylvania-Ohio border. Champ crosses into Ohio and proceeds to Lil Man's house in the woods. When he arrives, there are two mid-sized cars and a black Chevy Tahoe in the garage. Champ parks his bike and walks inside.

Once inside, he greets the top leaders and drug traffickers that he knows well. The money man, Red Eyes, is in the living room giving instructions to the muscle men, Blue and Big Boy. Darryl and a white female that Champ has never seen before sit on the couch and listen to Red Eyes speak. Champ does not interrupt. He knows his role, and stands quietly in the room to listen to what Red Eyes has to say.

"Blue, you take the silver rental and stay on call a few blocks away. If anything goes wrong, call Champ and get him the word. Champ and Big Boy, take the gold rental and pick up payments from the local boys. White Chocolate and I will deliver the package and return to the ranch to count," Red Eyes said in a serious tone. "Stay on schedule; we got eyes and ears on us. There is no room for mistakes," he added.

Everyone in the room nods their head and follows the instructions given. Champ and Big Boy take to the streets of Brownsville, the third-largest city in the state of Ohio, and the number one city for drug trafficking thanks to Red Eyes. Champ gets in and out of the car to collect bags of money, while Big Boy drove. At the final stop, Big Boy gets out of the car with Champ and gets into a black Lincoln with his wife. Champ takes the money and is headed to the stash spot, a live jazz club called the Fat Fish.

The Fat Fish jazz club is a popular night spot on the south side of Brownsville. It is two levels: the bottom floor has a live band

and a bar, and the second floor has a restaurant, a bar, and an outside balcony. Champ is enjoying fried fish when his cell phone rings.

"The feds got Red Eyes and they let the girl go. Get out of there right now," Blue's voice yelled into the cell phone.

Champ swallows hard. His face flushes and his head gets tight. He breathes deep as he looks quickly around the Fat Fish to see the exit. He walks downstairs, past the live band, to the men's bathroom. He is nervous. He splashes water on his face and vomits up his meal. He exits the bathroom and walks out the back service entrance to the parking garage. A young black man pulls his car into the garage and parks.

Champ takes out his gun and said, "Sorry, man, I need your clothes, only your clothes. I don't want to hurt you; I just need to change clothes."

The man strips and Champ runs off with his clothes. He runs two blocks and stops in an alley to change. Champ walks briskly and stops a taxi cab.

"East Brownsville please," Champ said. In the back seat of the cab, his mind is racing. He doesn't know where to go or who to trust. He gets out at a hotel and walks around the back of the building. He calls Big Boy's cell phone and gets no answer. He calls Big Boy's wife and gets no answer.

He checks into the hotel and sits down on the bed. He kept calling around to try to find out what happened. Finally, Big Boy calls his phone and said, "Yo, they got Red Eyes at the drop and let the white bitch go. They raided the ranch at the same time as they moved in at the mall. They raided your crib on the south side and the houses in the suburbs that your auntie is renting out. You better get out of town, man—they hot on us right now."

Champ hangs up and falls back on the bed. He stays in the hotel room for two nights and on the third day he calls Diamond from a pay phone and asks her to come and pick him up.

When Diamond pulls up to the spot where Champ is standing, she notices the sad look on his face. He gets into the truck and said, "Hey, lil momma, I'm happy to see you. Can you please take me to the airport; I have to try to get out of the country before the feds get me. They got my money man and I know they are looking for me right now."

"Okay, baby, anything that you need I will try my best to do it for you," Diamond replied.

"Take the back roads, baby; the main entrance to the airport is not safe for me to use. If I can get to the small private plane that is kept around back, I will be good. Will you call my brother Calvin for me? I need you to stop at locker 304 and use this key to open the door. There is $50,000 cash inside of the black bag. Get it to my brother and tell him to make sure he uses it to buy the music equipment that he needs to record his CD," Champ said as he hands her a small silver mailbox key.

"Okay, baby. Write the number on here," Diamond said as she gives Champ a small blue notepad and a pen to write. Diamond drives cautiously and slowly through the windy back roads that lead from Brownsville to the small private airport that Champ uses.

The rear entrance to the airport is a small dirt road that cut off of the main road and led to the control tower and storage units. The small white emergency plane came into view and Champ's heart fluttered.

"Baby, I'm sorry I'm running like this, but a caged bird is not free, and I'd rather live across the border than in prison for the rest of my life," Champ said.

"I know, baby. We can fight this thing once you are safe. We will find a way to handle this," Diamond said.

She stops the truck to let Champ out. He turns towards her and said, "Write down your address; we can communicate by letter, not by pones. I will give you instructions that way," he said.

Diamond scribbles her address on the small piece of paper and gives it to Champ. He kisses her lips and gets out of the truck. Diamond watches him as he disappears behind the storage units. She knows not to wait around the scene, so she backs the truck up and pulls off. She drives around the front entrance of the airport and parks in front of the baggage claim and locker area. She walks over to locker 304 and opens it. She struggles to remove the black bag full of money.

All the way home Diamond's mind races with thoughts. She knows she has access to the federal justice information system and that she can research his case. She knows that he trusts her to collect large amounts of money and direct the funds. She also knows that Champ's life is becoming her own and that soon all of his problems will become hers as well. But what she does not know is that her big brother is aware of her actions, and that he is about to get directly involved, too.

Chapter 22

When Diamond pulls up to her house, Junior is on the front porch waiting. Her heart drops and her stomach gets tight. She is anxious about confronting her brother because she knows it will be bad. She keeps her foot on the brake and stares at him. His face is tight and scowling. He is six feet four inches tall and 220 pounds. He has an almond complexion, half black and half Italian. He is handsome and vicious, protective and territorial. Diamond has an agreement with Junior and she never planned to break it. The consequences are going to be severe, violent even.

Diamond looks at her brother one last time and pulls off. She drives around back and down the alley to her house. She takes a deep breath and places the black money bag on the floor of the back seat. She gets out of the car and walks up the back steps onto the porch. She knows something bad is about to happen.

Junior opens the back door and meets her face to face. He grabs her by the face and by the hair. He grabs her body and pushes her into the house. She does not speak, but protects herself the best she can from his attack. He pins her against the wall and yells, while pointing his finger in her face.

"You are breaking all of the fucking rules, bitch!" Junior screamed. "You are going to get yourself killed. You are part of the college crowd, not the drug crowd. Are you fucking crazy? Are you a street whore tricking for cash? If you go near that nigger Champ again, I will cut you off and never speak to you again."

Diamond said nothing. He releases his grip and steps away from her. He stares at her and turns to walk away. She sits on the back porch and cries. She thinks about Champ and she wants to run away with him. She waits until Junior left to retrieve the money from the truck. She takes it to the safe in her closet and secures it inside. She takes a shower and lies on her bed. She is exhausted and needs to sleep.

She woke up early the next morning and dialed Calvin's phone number.

"Hello," his voice answered.

"Good morning. My name is Diamond and I need to meet you soon," she said.

"Do I know you? What did you say your name was, Diamond?" Calvin asked.

"Yes. I am your brother's girlfriend and I need to see you right away. Where are you?" Diamond asked.

"I live in South Carolina. Where are you?" he asked.

"I live in Pennsylvania. Can you come here? I can pay for a train ticket. Is your last name the same as your brother's?" she asked.

"Of course it is, we are of the same blood and fall from the same tree. I can come tomorrow night," he answered.

"Good. I will see you then," she said and hung up the phone.

She got on the computer and paid for his train ticket online. She lay back down and went to sleep. She did not leave her house until it was time to pick Calvin up from the train station.

Calvin is six feet and six inches tall. He has a high yellow complexion, with green eyes and a nice smile. He lives with his mother, a conniving woman. Champ supports his brother financially. Champ makes sure that Calvin picks up funds from the Western Union or Money Gram. Champ and Calvin remain close and talk on the phone.

Calvin moved to South Carolina with his mother shortly after Champ graduated from high school. Calvin went to high school and studied to become a licensed barber and a musician. Although Calvin and Champ shared the same life path growing up, they went in opposite directions. Champ took to the streets to make a living for himself and his brother, while Calvin went to school and was sheltered from the ills of the world.

Calvin has a selective memory about his mother and is not outwardly angry with her, but Champ on the other hand is very upset and shows his mother no respect. Calvin is a rapper and expresses himself through spoken word and rhymes. He attracts many lady friends, and has a set of twins by an older, married woman.

Diamond is parked in front of the train station leaning on her truck when Calvin exits. He looks just like Champ, but younger, and much taller.

Diamond walks towards him and said, "Hello, I'm Diamond. It's very nice to meet you."

"Wow, shorty, nice to meet you too," he replied.

"Let's go," Diamond said walking to her truck.

Calvin gets into the passenger side and she pulls off.

"So what's up? Where's my brother?" he asked.

"He's gone. Let's talk about it over dinner, okay," Diamond said.

Calvin nods his head and sits back in the seat. Diamond drives across town to her favorite Jamaican restaurant.

Once inside, Diamond explains to Calvin, "Your brother is in Canada. He cannot come back to the states anytime soon. He has some money for you and he wants you to invest it in music equipment and studio time."

"How much money?" he asked.

"Fifty grand," she answered.

"What? Are you serious?" Calvin asked with excitement. He cannot sit still. He moves around in his chair like an antsy child waiting for something.

"Will you come back to my house so that we can figure it out?" she asked.

"Hell yes, you just made my day. Can we call my brother?" he asked.

"Nope, he will write to me soon and I will get you the address then," Diamond said.

"Cool, let's eat and celebrate. This is a good day," Calvin said with a smile.

Diamond agreed. They ate and had drinks and celebrated. Diamond was a little tipsy when they left the restaurant, so she had to drive home slow.

"So why did my brother have to leave?" Calvin asked.

"Can we please wait until we get to my house, because I can't talk and drive right now," she said as she gripped the steering wheel with both hands.

"Sure. Are you okay? Do you want me to drive?" Calvin asked,

"No, I'm good. I live close by," Diamond said as she focused on the road.

Calvin sat back and watched the scenery as she drove home slowly. She pulled the truck in front of her house and parked. It was late afternoon and Lynne wasn't home. Diamond and Calvin went into the house and downstairs to the basement. She fell on the love seat and he sat in a chair.

"So what happened to my brother?" Calvin asked.

"I don't know exactly what happened, but I do know that he can't come back home anytime soon. He's on the run and I think his partners are in jail," Diamond confessed.

"It's always something going on with my brother. He works hard to provide for me. I wish there was something that I could do," Calvin said.

"You can do what he asked you to do and get your music equipment and studio time," she advised.

"Yeah, you're right. I remember the first rhyme that I wrote. I was in like the eighth grade and my mom made me go to bed early one night. I woke up in the middle of the night to get something to drink and I heard my mom having sex with her boyfriend. I was pissed and I went into the bathroom, locked the door, and wrote my first rhyme about death and murder. I really wanted to kill the both of them," Calvin confessed.

"That's tough to deal with. Are you and your brother close?" she asked.

"He is five years older than I am, but yes, we are close. I remember him walking me to the bus stop each morning for school. He had to be in like the tenth grade, smoking weed at the bus stop. We used to sleep in the same bed. He would sneak out the window at night and I would have to wake up to let him back in the window. We lived in the mountains of West Virginia, so there was a creek outside our window. The sound of the rushing water was calming to me," Calvin admitted.

"Are you and your mom close?" Diamond asked.

"I love her and I would do anything for her, but she is a sneaky woman. We moved around a lot. I got used to meeting new people and developed the art of conversation. Mommy is a hustler too, so I got good at listening to and reading people," Calvin said.

"How old was Champ when he first started taking care of you?" Diamond asked.

"My brother always took care of me. My mom would leave us in the house alone for two and three days at a time. My brother would get me up and dressed and off to school. He would cook for me and make sure I got all of my homework done. After my mom left, and we went to live with my aunt Angela and uncle Von, my brother changed. It was around the same time that my uncle took basketball from him, maybe eleventh grade. I used to make runs for him. I would go to the spot and collect the money and once I was safe, he would come behind me and deliver the drugs. I didn't understand it then because I was a kid. But once I got older, I realized that the house we lived in was not our own and that my mom was off doing her own thing. I have never wanted or needed for anything, and I'm glad my brother sacrificed himself to make a way for me," Calvin said.

"Do you smoke too?" she asked.

"Sure do, all day long. Do you?" he asked.

"No, I've never had the desire to smoke. I'm a lady!" she answered.

"So what's up with the fifty grand?" he asked.

"I have it. What do you think is the safest way to get you home?" she asked.

"My brother always told me to take myself, so I think driving back down south would be best," Calvin said.

"Me too; I have to go to school for summer classes soon so we will have to leave early in the morning," Diamond said.

"Cool," Calvin said.

Diamond and Calvin spent the rest of the night talking. The next morning they drove down south. Diamond didn't stay, she turned right around and drove back home so that she could get ready to go back to school for summer classes to start.

Chapter 23

Calvin went straight to the music store with the money Champ gave him. He bought a MPC 2000 XL; a sixteen-track digital recorder; a Yamaha Motif 8; a 102-track recorder; and a microphone. Calvin soundproofed his bedroom and worked with his homeboy Chaz to make beats. Calvin and Chaz became locally known and caught the attention of a small management company, Southern Records Inc. The manager signed Calvin and Chaz to a three-year contract, and they performed all over the south at clubs and local events. One song, "Put Your Hands Up," was used in a commercial, but Calvin was never paid. Calvin, Chaz, and their manager were on bad terms when Calvin decided to go to California to do a private show.

When Calvin steps off the airplane in Los Angeles, California, the air is hot and humid. The sun is shining bright and Calvin lifts his face to the sky and smiles.

"Hey, man, over here," a man's voice calls out. It is Ron G,

Calvin's producer friend. Calvin spots him and walks towards him.

"Hey, man, how are you?" Ron G said as Calvin approaches.

"Better now that I'm here. So what's up with the show tonight?" Calvin asked.

"It's on. I'm going to take you to your hotel room to change and then we will go straight to the club," Ron G said.

The two men load Calvin's bags into the taxi and pull off into the airport traffic. Calvin and Ron G drive to the Hilton Hotel to change clothes and leave back out to travel downtown Los Angeles. Club Ecstasy is not open to the public when they arrive. Inside the club the waiters and club workers prepare for the crowd. Ron G walks over to the stage and shakes hands with a middle-aged black man. Calvin follows.

"This is Young Calvin, a new rapper from the south," Ron G said.

"Good to meet you. Come up on stage and run through your songs a few times," the man said to Calvin.

"Songs?" Calvin asked Ron G.

"Yeah, my man is going to let you perform two songs tonight. So go ahead and take the stage, brother," Ron G said. Calvin hops on stage and takes the microphone in his hand.

"Check one-two, check one-two," he said.

The middle-aged black man stands behind the curtain on the stage and adjusts the volume of the microphone and dims the lights. Ron G mans the DJ booth and puts on a beat. Calvin performs his two songs with energy and excitement. Ron G and the club staff are nodding their heads and moving to the music. They applaud when Calvin is done. Ron G and Calvin sit at the bar and have a drink.

"Hey, man, you really are talented. Me and you could hit up a couple more clubs over the next week and get your music out," Ron G said.

"Yeah, that would be cool. I planned to stay about a week anyway," Calvin replied. The two men finish their drinks and walk backstage to get ready for the show.

Backstage is two small dressing rooms, a lounge with a private bar, and the control room where the stage manager works. Calvin chills in the lounge and watches as the waitresses and club girls come to work through the back door.

Just then, Shante, a tall, thick, brown-skinned hostess, walks through the back door. She wears a tight black tank top with a short denim skirt and black fishnet stockings. Her black heels make her taller than the other girls. Calvin stands up as soon as she walks in his direction.

"Hello, shorty. What's your name?" Calvin said with a smile.

Shante smiles back and said, "Shorty? Where are you from?"

"I'm from the south. Are you going to tell me your name?" Calvin asked.

"My name is Shante and I'm from the Bahamas. I attend college here in L.A. I'm studying to be an actress," she said.

"I'm Calvin and I'm performing tonight. Maybe we can hang out when you get off work," Calvin said.

"Yeah, maybe. I have to get to work. I'll see you later. Good luck tonight, handsome," she said.

"Thanks," he said.

Shante walks towards the front of the club and out of Calvin's sight. It is 7:00 p.m. and the DJ starts the music. People start to come inside and slowly Club Ecstasy comes alive.

Ron G comes backstage and said, "You go on at 9:00 p.m. Do you want to chill until then? Or do you want to get some fresh air outside?"

"Fresh air sounds good," Calvin said.

"Cool, let's roll; I got a friend out back waiting," Ron G said.

Calvin and Ron G walk out the back door and get into the Chevy Caprice that is waiting in the alley behind the club. Inside the car are two women. Ron G introduced them, "This is Shay and that is La La."

"Nice to meet you, ladies," Calvin said.

"These ladies have party supplies for us, man. The finest Cali buds, a few pills, and some coke if you get high," Ron G said.

"No, thanks. I got my own green," Calvin answered.

"Yeah, well that's cool. But you see these pills right here? These are called Superman because you fly high on them," Ron G said.

"I'm good, man, honestly. Matter of fact I'm going to go back inside," Calvin said as he opens the car door and walks back into the club.

Calvin walks around the club, observing the activities. Shante is at the front door checking the identification of the people coming in. Calvin sits at the bar and has a drink as the club becomes packed with people. At 8:50 p.m. the same middle-aged black man takes the stage to introduce Calvin. "Tonight is a special night, L.A. We have an extraordinary MC visiting us from the dirty south. Please join me in welcoming to the stage Young Calvin."

The crowd claps as Calvin steps onto the stage to perform. The DJ starts the beat and Calvin raps with more energy and excitement than before. He moves quickly from one end of the stage to the other. He waves his hands and gets the crowd involved. After the show, the crowd screams and Calvin exits to go backstage and chill out. Shante comes backstage with a big smile on her face.

"Hey, you are really good! We need you out here more often," she said.

"Thanks," Calvin said and smiled.

"Come in here, I want to show you something," Shante said as she walks towards one of the dressing rooms. Calvin follows.

"Welcome to Club X," Shante said as she holds out her tongue with a small while pill on the tip.

Calvin backs up and said, "I don't do pills, shorty, only bud for me."

"Live a little, tonight is the only night we may have to kick it," Shante said.

Calvin leans forward and kisses her. He takes the pill from her tongue and swallows. He has already had a few drinks and is tipsy. Shante takes out a pill for herself and swallows. Both of them walk to the private bar backstage for a drink.

"Drink plenty of water now; no more alcohol tonight," Shante said.

"Okay, and what am I supposed to do for the rest of the night?" Calvin asked.

"Give me twenty minutes and I'll be back. Sit in the lounge until your pill kicks in," Shante said as she hurries away.

Calvin falls back onto the couch and chills out. He closes his eyes and listens to the music. Suddenly, he feels euphoric and happy. The music becomes intoxicating as he sits, smiling, bobbing his head and tapping his feet. He is excited and wants to dance. Just as he stands to go to the dance floor, Shante comes backstage.

She looks like a goddess walking towards him. He moves towards her and they stand face to face dancing to the music. She is sexy and exotic, he is sensual and erotic. Their bodies complement each other as they dance. Shante's body is hot as she grinds to the beat. She can feel Calvin's manhood in his jeans. She takes Calvin by his hand and leads him to the same dressing room that they popped the pills in.

She locks the door and said to Calvin, "I don't know you well, but I like you. It's been a few months since me and my man broke up and I want to please myself tonight."

"How exactly would you like to please yourself?" Calvin asked.

"By pleasing you, so pull down your jeans, Southern boy, and let me blow your mind," Shante said.

Calvin nods his head and unbuckles his belt and pants. Shante takes over and satisfies him. When she is finished, he looks at her and smiles.

"If you give me a few minutes, I will get my home girl to finish my shift so we can go back to my apartment for the night," Shante said.

"You got it. I'll get myself together and wait in the lounge," Calvin replied.

Shante leaves the dressing room and Calvin looks at himself in the mirror and said, "Do you like what you see? Getting blown by bitches in Cali, rocking clubs and popping E. Damn, I love me."

Shante comes right back and knocks on the door. She asked, "Are you ready to tour Cali with me? I'm fucking with you heavy tonight."

"Let's roll, shorty, you got it," Calvin replied.

Shante and Calvin catch a cab to her apartment and shack up for the night. They explore each other's private places and fall asleep. Calvin sleeps late the next day; between the traveling, the show, the pill, and the sex, he is tired. Shante is gone when he sits up in her bed. He calls Ron G on his cell phone.

"Yo, man, what's up?" Calvin asked.

"Hey, man, where are you? I came backstage and you were gone," Ron G said.

"I'm safe. I'll meet you at the hotel later. Did you get another spot for tonight?" Calvin asked.

"You know I got your back. We have a show at Club 98 at 10:00 tonight. I'll meet you at your room about 7:00 p.m.," Ron G said.

"Cool, see you then," Calvin said and hung up the phone. He has no idea where he is or how to get back to his hotel room. He walks to the refrigerator to get something to drink when Shante came home.

"Hi. Did you sleep well?" she asked.

"Yep. How about you? Did you sleep well?" Calvin asked.

"I'm well rested. I don't work tonight, so I thought we could hang out," Shante said.

"I have another show at Club 98 tonight," Calvin answered.

"It's cool, that club will be live tonight. My homeboy is a bouncer there. I'll meet you there. What time do you go on?" Shante asked.

"I go on at 10:00 p.m. Meet me at the bar after I'm done and we can kick it," Calvin said.

"Okay, let me get you across town to your room," Shante said.

Calvin gathers his belongings and let Shante drive him to his room.

Later that night at Club 98, Calvin rocks the stage. The crowd embraces his conscious rap style. He is unique and a pleasure to listen to. Shante is infatuated with the thought of being his lady because she can see that he is a winner. She can see riches and fame for him and even though she has her own dreams of being an actress, she wants him and all that he embodies.

After the show, Shante sits at the bar and waits for Calvin to meet her. She wants to take a pill and take Calvin home.

"Hey there, beautiful, what are you drinking on?" Calvin asked Shante as he joins her.

"Hey there, handsome, that was a great show! You look hella good on that stage rhyming. Tall, green eyes, voice raspy from smoking," Shante replied.

Calvin is caught off guard. Shante has flavor. Her slight island accent, her height, five feet seven inches, her caramel brown skin, long dark brown hair, apple bottom, and coke bottle shape. She has a thin waist and a cute face. She is a college girl by day and on the club scene at night.

But what Calvin doesn't know is that she is addicted to pills and eats one at least every other night. She is strong and sexy outside, but inside she is a zombie. She is reckless and makes poor decisions.

Calvin and Shante become a couple quick. She shows him around L.A. and introduces him to people. He requires her presence at each show. She is his fly girl.

Calvin is building a career rapping and is booked to do live shows across the United States. Shante stays in L.A. while Calvin travels and is surrounded by the music industry's vultures, the men and women he parties with, pops pills with, performs with, and sleeps with.

One night at a party in Atlanta, Georgia, Calvin wants to get high, but these people don't do pills. Calvin is introduced to cocaine: the dream, Go Fast, China White, the devil. The first time is the last time for Calvin. He overdoses and is rushed to the emergency room.

Calvin is high and out of his mind. He is cold and he sees demons in the faces of the doctors and nurses that treat him. He has to be strapped to the hospital bed and physically restrained. He speaks in tongues and recites biblical verses. He flat lines and his heartbeat stops. He lies lifeless on the hospital bed as the doctors and nurses scramble to give him shock treatment to restart his heart.

As the doctor shocks him the first time, his body jerks up and falls back down on the bed. No heart beat. The second time, the doctor increases the voltage, and shocks him. No heartbeat. At that moment Calvin hears a deep voice inside of him say, "My child, rise. It is not your time." The very drugs that Champ sold to provide for Calvin nearly killed him.

Chapter 24

After seven days, Calvin gets out of the hospital and goes back home to live with his mother down south. Calvin calls Diamond and asks for his brother's address. He tells her all about his travels to L.A. and his near-death experience. Diamond gives him the address and Calvin writes his brother a letter that read,

"Champ, hey big brother, how are you? Man, I've been going through some things and I need to talk to you. I did what you asked me to do and I got all of the equipment that I needed. Thanks. I'm thankful to have a brother like you. You have always had my back. I am ashamed to tell you, but I recently overdosed on cocaine and I just got out of the hospital. I'm back at home with Mom, but I really need to see you. Be safe and write back soon. Love, Calvin."

Champ read the letter and an overwhelming feeling of guilt came over him. He became depressed, angry, and sad. For the first time in his life he is taking a timeout to reflect on all that he has done. He realizes that the same love that he lacks from his mother he finds in the streets. He realizes that he helps to ruin many families across the states by selling poison to the mothers and fathers, aunts, uncles, and grandparents of the children.

He is pissed that his father isn't man enough to be around and that his mother is bold enough to have left her children behind. His brother is his inspiration and he feels terrible that he cannot protect him.

To cope with his stress, Champ starts to walk the hemp fields daily to find peace. He talks to the plants, he lifts weights, and smokes bud. He sits still and starts to hear a small voice inside of him. He cries out to God and falls on his knees to pray.

For the first time since he was a child, he is reading the Bible and praying that his soul will be cleansed. He has a clear vision for his life as a hemp farmer and he knows that he has to get Diamond and Calvin to Canada with him so that they will all be out of sight of the authorities.

During all of the madness, Diamond returns to college for summer classes. In order to be productive she visits the library and accesses the criminal justice information system and works on collecting information on Champ's case.

She has made a mess of her life: Junior has cut her off and will not speak to her, Champ is in another country thousands of miles away, and Calvin is recovering from a drug overdose and depression. Diamond knows that she cannot afford to become distracted by all that surrounds her, so once again she buries herself in her school work, almost living in the library, and keeping to herself.

Each day after class Diamond studies and completes her assignments, and then she sits down at the computer to record all of the details of Champ's case. She starts to ask questions of the law professors on campus and conducts research on the federal drug laws.

By the end of the summer Diamond feels confident that if she can find the right attorney to give the information to, then Champ may be able to beat the case. She learns through her research that Red Eyes was convicted of drug trafficking and conspiracy charges and received a sentence of twenty-seven years in federal prison. She also learned that the feds have no physical evidence on Champ, only surveillance footage and pictures of him with known drug traffickers, as well as illegal wire taps on their cell phones that discussed, in code, drug deals and large amounts of money.

But because Champ was never around when the drug deals went down and because the wire taps were illegal, none of the evidence obtained from them was admissible in court. She read that Canada did not deport American citizens back to the states for nonviolent criminal charges, and since Champ was being investigated for drug trafficking charges and not actually charged, he was safe in Canada.

Diamond finishes her summer classes and returns to Valley. Lynne is at home when Diamond walks into the house. Lynne is singing and packing a suitcase.

"Where are you going?" Diamond asked.

"Honey, sit down, we need to talk," Lynne said.

"Oh, no. What's up, Mommy?" Diamond asked as she follows her mother to the kitchen table.

"Well, sweetie, your father and I have been divorced for about fifteen years now and out of respect for you and your brother, I have not had another man live in our home. Diamond, you are a young woman now, a college student, and I have waited a very long time for love. I am dating a wonderful man from Virginia and I am going to stay at his house on the beach for a week," Lynne said.

"Okay, Mom, so you have a man, what's the big deal?" Diamond replied.

Lynne smiles and said, "The big deal is that I am considering moving to Virginia and getting re-married this winter."

"Moving? Re-married? How long have you known this man?" Diamond questioned.

"Baby, Paul and I have been together for about a year now. I met him last summer at the jazz festival in Ohio. He has a daughter the same age as you and he's been divorced for about five years now. He's a hardworking man and he will take good care of me," Lynne said.

"Wow, I've been so caught up at school that I didn't even notice that you were in love. This is crazy, first Champ leaves and now you, too. So what's going to happen to the house?" Diamond asked.

"The house will be fine. Your brother can keep up with it. I haven't moved yet; I'm just visiting right now. I just wanted to share my plans with you. Wherever I go, you are always welcome," Lynne said with a smile.

"Thanks, Mommy. I'm going to go to my room for a while. Let me know when you are about to leave," Diamond said as she gets up from the table and kisses her mother on the forehead.

"I'm not leaving until morning, baby, but I will be sure to let you know," Lynne said.

Diamond walks to her room to think. She lies across her bed and turns on some music. So many things are on her mind so she decides to write Champ a letter.

"Hi baby, my mom just told me that she might be moving down south with her new man. You are there and I am here. I feel lonely. School is great and I have a lot of information for you. Maybe I can visit you while I wait for school to start again. I hope all is well with you. I love you."

Diamond seals the letter, puts a stamp on it, and walks outside to drop it in the mailbox. Calvin crosses her mind and decides to go to her room and call him.

"Hello," Calvin answered.

"Hi, it's Diamond. How are you?" she asked.

"I'm good, just taking it one day at a time. Have you heard from my brother? I want to talk to him," Calvin said.

"I'm thinking about going to visit him soon. Do you want to go?" Diamond asked.

"Yes. I need to see him soon. He helps me to stay focused," Calvin said.

"I heard that there was going to be an international film festival up north next week and they are still looking to book spoken word poets to perform. Are you interested?" Diamond asked.

"Sure. I haven't been on stage since I overdosed. It would be good for me to get away to see my brother and do a show," Calvin replied.

"Okay, I am going to be your manager for this trip and register you for the show. I'm also going to book our flights for tomorrow night. You can fly from there and I will fly from here and we will meet in New York. I will call you back with the information," Diamond said.

"Cool. I'll start packing right away," Calvin said and hung up the phone.

Diamond sits at her computer and makes the reservations. She prints out the information and calls Calvin back.

"Hey, your flight leaves at 8:00 p.m. and arrives at 11:00 p.m. I will leave at 8:00 p.m. and arrive at 10:00 p.m.. I will pick up the rental car and wait for you at your baggage claim area," Diamond said.

"Okay. Be safe," Calvin said.

She feels better now, and is looking forward to spending time with Champ. She gets back online and registers Calvin for the show. She is excited as she empties her suitcases from summer school and re-packs her bags for Canada.

The next morning Lynne and Diamond say their good-byes and Lynne leaves for Virginia. Diamond walks downstairs to the bathroom in the basement to retrieve the money that Champ gave her. She takes the money to her room and separates it into small piles.

Once the money is separate, she gets in her truck and drives around town to the local banks to purchase travelers checks in denominations of $500 each. It takes her all day to drive from bank to bank. She is able to get $25,000 in travelers checks to carry with her. She secures the rest of the money in a safe deposit box at the bank where she has an account. Since Lynne isn't at home, she won't want to take the chance of leaving the money unattended.

The next night, Diamond flies to New York, rents a car, and waits for Calvin's flight to land. Calvin exits the airplane and walks to the baggage claim area. Just as he comes into Diamond's view, two white men walk along each side of him.

"Mr. Woods, please come with us," one man said.

Calvin looks at the men and keeps walking.

"Mr. Woods, we are federal agents and we are looking for your brother Champ," the same man said.

Calvin's heart beat faster as he continues to walk towards the baggage claim area. Diamond watches from a distance as the two men put their arms on each one of Calvin's arms and escort him away. Diamond follows.

Inside of a small airport security room, the two agents question Calvin about his destination and Champ.

"When was the last time you saw your brother?" one man asked.

"A few years ago," Calvin answered.

"Do you know where he is now?" the man asked.

"No. I have not seen my brother or heard from him," Calvin answered. Just then there is a knock at the door. One agent opens it and Diamond walks in.

"Good evening, gentlemen. My name is Ms. Smith and Mr. Woods is my client. We have a show in New York City tonight and we must be going. Now, if you don't have any official charges or reason to detain Mr. Woods, we would appreciate his immediate release," Diamond said with confidence and authority. Both agents look at each other and whisper amongst themselves.

One man looks at Calvin and said, "Your brother is under investigation and we need to speak to him right away. We will be watching you and your family very closely until we find him. Please know that once we find him, he is finished."

Calvin glares at the man and said nothing. He stands up and walks towards the door where Diamond is standing. She exits first, followed by Calvin and the two men.

Diamond stops to address the two agents. "Gentlemen, there is a fine line between investigation and harassment. Please be mindful of that the next time you detain my client."

The two men laugh at Diamond and one said, "Young lady, please be careful. If you lay with dogs you just might catch fleas."

Diamond and Calvin leave the airport and drive to the Canadian border. The border patrol question them, check their identification, walk a drug dog around the car, and let them cross the border. Diamond follows the highway signs to Niagara Falls. She parks in the same parking lot that Davion parked in before and dials his number.

"Hello," Davion answered.

"Hi, it's Diamond. I'm here in Canada and I'm at the falls. Will you come and get me and take me to the farm?" she asked.

"Sure thing, cousin; give me about thirty minutes and meet me at the same spot we parked last time," Davion said.

"I'm already there. See you soon," Diamond said and hung up the phone.

"I want to see the falls at night. Let's get out and walk," Calvin said.

Diamond and Calvin walk the same path that she and Champ walked before. The mist of the falls feels refreshing on her face and the sound of the rushing water makes her feel at peace.

"This is amazing. The height and power of the water, and the colors reflecting off the water at the bottom," Calvin said as he gazed at the falls.

"This is heaven, safe from all harm and with family," Diamond replied.

"Thanks for getting us here, my brother is important to me," Calvin said.

"Yes, he is a special man and I love him very much. You should do well at the festival, I hear there will be major international producers and music industry reps there," she said.

"Rhyming is self-expression, and I have something to say," Calvin said.

At that moment, Diamond considers that she is not going back home. Calvin can perform in Canada, Europe, and overseas. She can finish college here and practice law if she wants to. Or she can help Champ with the hemp farm and start a business of her

own. The one thing that she knows for sure is that she will marry Champ and use all of her knowledge to protect him. In return, Champ will love and honor her for the rest of their lives.

About the Author

Monique, born and raised in concentrated poverty and the shadows of the old steel mill city of Farrell, Pennsylvania, currently works as an educator and mentor to at-risk youth in Washington, D.C. She holds a BA in sociology from Georgia State University in Atlanta, Georgia. While at Georgia State, Monique studied the impact of race and ethnicity, poverty, and the disparities in the United States education system.

Monique is currently earning her master's degree in teaching from Bowie State University in Bowie, Maryland. Her teaching experience includes tutoring at-risk youth in Decatur, Georgia; teaching critical thinking skills to Upward Bound students in Atlanta, Georgia; teaching SAT prep to Upward Bound students at the University of Maryland, College Park; and teaching math and science to emotionally disturbed youth in Washington, D.C.

Monique is dedicated to making a positive difference in the lives of today's youth and hopes to prove that no matter how difficult life may be, success is possible with hard work and perseverance.